A MURDER OF CROWS

Richard Barrett

5-15-2011

ATHENA PRESS
LONDON

A MURDER OF CROWS
Copyright © Richard Barrett 2003

All Rights Reserved

No part of this book may be reproduced in any form
by photocopying or by any electronic or mechanical means,
including information storage or retrieval systems,
without permission in writing from both the copyright
owner and the publisher of this book.

ISBN 1 84401 079 1

First Published 2003 by
ATHENA PRESS
Queen's House, 2 Holly Road
Twickenham, TW1 4EG
United Kingdom

Printed for Athena Press

A MURDER OF CROWS

To Diane, Billy and Kate, and everybody else who provided inspiration or support (if you don't know who you are, I'm sure I'll get around to telling you.)

These will be the days that we'll remember in days to come
The years slip by so quickly now we're none of us so young...
...And if I dream, it'll be of you, of you, old friend...

Tom Robinson, *Old Friend*.

And when the soldier did awaken to find the world not fit for heroes to live in his misery was shackled upon him beyond the power of immediate revolt. Poor fool, he had been blinded into thinking that the right to... create children rather than destroy human beings... was heaven enough.

John A. Lee, *Soldier*.

Tomorrow came and went, yesterday fades, it echoes in the shadows.

Title of a painting by Annette Fry.

Contents

Prologue   9

Part One
Remembering Kirsty

Gone Away, Gone Away, He Said   21
The Whartons   29
Years That Slipped By Quickly   34
Jacqui   37
Rex   40
Interlude   45

Part Two
The Real Kirsty

Back Stories   51
The Disappeared One   64
Death   67
Chilli, Wine and Suspicions   72
A World Fit For Heroes To Live In 76
Glamis   82
In The Midst Of Life   86
Sharon   94

The Educator	100
Just A Quick Chat	108
Interlude	110

Part Three
What Became Of Kirsty

Revelations	117
I Can Still Get Angry, Even Now I Know She's Dead	123
Coffee Morning	138
Tim	147
Echoing In The Shadows	149

PROLOGUE

1st July 1916

Sandy Crow knew that he had been sent to the Somme to die.

He stood holding his rifle, with fixed bayonet, waiting to go over the top. Sam King and Duncan Ogilvie, on either side of him, were doing the same thing, as were the rest of the platoon.

Sandy felt himself begin to sweat as their personal zero hour approached. His seventy pounds of equipment and the warm morning sun may have been partially responsible for this; it was going to be a lovely day. On a quiet sector such as this one had been, it was possible to enjoy lovely days. Almost. Not today though. Today was going to be different.

There was no pretence now that the Germans had all been destroyed by the bombardment that had stretched continuously across the last week of June. Their machine gun and artillery fire were proof enough of that. In one minute's time, Sandy's wave was due to leave the assault trench and face them.

He was the only man in his platoon who had been in an action such as this before, at Loos, the previous September. He had arrived in France just in time for that. Most of his original mates had become part of the casualty lists during that battle, and the remainder of them had been broken up and scattered amongst the newer battalions – promoted, in many cases – to provide them with at least a few experienced men.

It almost made Sandy laugh sometimes; nineteen years old, in the midst of all these soldiers in their twenties, thirties and forties, and he was seen as the experienced one.

At the front of the trench, Sergeant Hay turned to face them.

'Good luck, lads,' he said, his narrow eyes travelling along the rows of volunteers, with their final cigarettes, rosary beads and photographs of loved ones. His gaze rested briefly on Sandy, as if to emphasise that he was even including him.

Hay had been made a sergeant on the grounds of civilian leadership experience – Sandy had heard that he had been a foreman in one of the distilleries – he had not fought in a battle before and it was obvious that he did not like having a kid under him who had. He had made that perfectly clear.

Don't start being decent just because you're scared shitless, Sandy thought. *I don't wish you good luck, you bastard.*

Lieutenant Carter blew his whistle. That was it. They began to climb the ladders, clearing the way for the portion of the next wave which would soon be moving up to replace them.

Sandy found himself pushed to the back a little, as he waited to get onto a ladder. This did not bother him. He wasn't in a hurry.

Then he was over, they all were, past their own barbed wire and marching, as they had been ordered to, into the hail of bullets and shells. Duncan Ogilvie went down almost immediately. Knowing that nobody was allowed to stop and help the wounded, Sandy had to make do with a quick backward glance. Even after a few yards though, he was unable to tell which khaki clad form was his friend. Behind him and as far ahead and to each side as he could see, the ground was covered with bodies, some still and silent, others writhing and screaming. They had to pick their way between, and sometimes over, them. In many places, blood was soaking into the soil. They were passed by walking wounded, and those who could only manage to crawl back to their own lines. Then there were some who did not appear to be injured at all, just crazy with terror, also making their way back.

Bloody hell, Sandy thought. It already seemed worse than Loos. He remembered the first day there and the two enemy soldiers he had bayoneted. The only two, so far. It was hard to believe that he would get close enough to any of them to do that today.

The bombardment seemed to come out of nowhere. Sandy was thrown several feet, landing on top of a corpse. He knew immediately that he was only winded, the impact had been well to one side of him. He sprang off the dead man as soon as he had his breath back, but remained in a crouch, looking about himself through the clearing smoke. Where were the others? Some had probably been blown out of existence and the rest must have kept walking.

Then, as he reached out and picked up his Lee Enfield, he spotted Sergeant Hay. He could hear him too, screaming above the shellfire and the chatter of machine guns. His thin, moustached face was contorted in agony and his leg was a bloody mess.

Sandy smiled.

*

1st July 1986

Sandy Crow looked out across a grey North Sea.

The Somme. A whole lifetime ago, even if it did sometimes seem so recent. July the First had proven itself an impossible date to forget, and year after year, more often than not, he had found himself thinking about the events of that terrible day on their anniversary.

Despite everything else, it was always Hay who came to mind first. The bastard had hated him. One of those unpleasant situations where a person who has power over you does not trouble to hide their dislike. One of Sandy's teachers had been like that as well.

Kirsty had had a similar problem at school one year.

She had eventually confided it to him, rather than any other member of the family. He had been flattered and had been able to offer her empathy, but no practical solutions.

She was in some kind of trouble now.

'What you thinking about, Grandad?'

She must have slipped into the room – the living room of the boarding house that had been his home for the past thirty-two years – at the same time that she was running through his mind. He often failed to realise that people were there when he was sitting looking out of his favourite window; his hearing was not the best any more. Not that it had ever been what it once was after all those shells during his three months on the Somme, before he got his Blighty One. Perhaps that weeklong bombardment which they had used as a curtain raiser to the battle had caused significant damage on its own.

'July the First thoughts?' Kirsten guessed. 'It's seventy years today, isn't it?'

'You don't forget much, do you?' Sandy gazed fondly up at her. 'Lass with a mind like yours ought to be off getting a bit more education, no' hanging around here. You need it nowadays.'

'Maybe one day. What's on your mind, Grandad? That stuff you told me a couple of years ago?'

'No, no, other things!'

It was bad enough; he felt now, that he had made her a party to that knowledge. He was not about to admit that it was something which still bothered him sometimes.

God, she was lovely, he thought. Her long, thin black hair and large brown eyes, that orphan of the storm look that she had always had, but which, at seventeen, she had really grown into. None of his other eight grandchildren meant as much to him as she did. If only her parents were capable of appreciating her for the special person that she was.

'Don't you go worrying about what I told you' he advised her. 'That's war for you – let's hope none of you ever go through one. It's not something I ever told anyone else, not even Marion or your dad or the others. I think I just wanted someone to know. I won't be around much longer, after all.'

'You?' Kirsten laughed. 'You'll outlive us all, you will.'

*

Two miles away, Rex Wharton was sitting at a window looking out to sea as well. His cottage, just outside Craigston, had become his refuge from the world ever since they told him that he would never play professionally again. That had been the saving grace of an otherwise unbearable situation, having somewhere like this to retreat to, in the country which his forebears had lived in. His father's forebears.

Rex had little enough else to celebrate about his life, since it had turned to shit. His wise investments perhaps; he had had the best possible financial adviser when he began to make decent money. Thanks to Dad, he was out of the game at twenty-two with a decent fucking nest egg behind him. He had that, but unfortunately, he didn't have Dad any more. No other family either, the way he was feeling about them. His friends were all hundreds of miles away and he was having a break from women. That was a very different scene when you were no longer playing; not that he had ever wanted a serious relationship with the sort of woman who hung around footballers.

Still, he had his home. It was a little large to realistically be described as a cottage, even though the estate agent had done precisely that. Made of the attractive local red sandstone, it was nearly a century old and perfect for Rex. He would not have wanted to be left rattling around in a mansion, even if he could have afforded one.

A knocking sounded at the front door. Who the hell was that? He couldn't think of anybody around here who could possibly have an interesting reason to visit him. He had not been bothered by salespeople or Jehovah's Witnesses up here so far, but if this was the beginning of it, he'd soon tell them to piss off. When he grew tired of his splendid isolation, he was capable of finding company for himself; he did not need it to come calling.

Leaving his couch, opposite the picture-frame window which overlooked the sea, Rex walked, with only a suggestion of a limp, up the hall.

'Hi,' Tim greeted him, as he opened the door.

'What are you doing here?'

'You're my brother. I've come to see you. I needed a break.'

'Oh yeah?' Rex curled his lip. 'Gets tiring pissing Dad's business away inch by inch, does it?'

Tim sighed. It did not look as if showing up in person like this was going to make the slightest difference.

'Look, Rex, I'm not asking to stay; I'm at a boarding house back in the town. Nearly didn't come out here at all.'

'That wasn't such a bad idea. Plenty of other interesting places to see round here. Grandma grew up here – that ought to mean something. There's loads of nice spots you could go and look at...this just isn't one of them.'

'So you don't want me to come in?' Tim asked, inviting Rex to spell it out.

'No. I'd've got in touch with you if I'd wanted to. I'm the one with a car and lots of fucking time on my hands, after all – I don't know how you can justify sloping off like this, wasting money in boarding houses!'

'I knew this'd be a waste of bloody time.'

Tim turned to leave and Rex immediately slammed the door.

★

Kirsten sat on the front doorstep of the Callum Brae guesthouse, enjoying her cigarette and the salt air. She was not allowed to smoke in the family's private living quarters, now that both of her parents had stopped. Sandy, incredibly, for a member of his generation, in this area, had given up in his sixties, so Kirsten was in a minority amongst the Crows. She intended to remain that way; tobacco was not a habit she expected to kick any time soon.

She spotted Tim Wharton sauntering towards her and smiled as she blew smoke into the High Street. What would her mother say if she knew that she had become intimately involved with one of the guests? Tim was a lot of fun, and it was nice to be with somebody kind, for a change. Tonight was going to be good. A thrill ran through Kirsten as she imagined herself showing Tim her tattoo.

How had it gone with the crocked footballer brother, she wondered? She had never met the town's celebrity resident, but everybody was talking about him, although they tended to refer to him as 'Rex Whatsisname'; his name had not got to the point of being a household word.

Bit of a wanker by all accounts, especially Tim's. The classic tall, dark and handsome midfielder, they said. That had never been Kirsten's sort of thing at all.

'Hiya,' she said, as Tim reached her.

'Hi.'

They kissed briefly outside the boarding house's front door and spent a minute sharing what was left of the cigarette.

'Away up to your room,' said Kirsten, flicking the stub towards the gutter. 'I'll be along soon. But it's bad news for smokers, I'm afraid.'

'What do you mean?'

'My mate Jacqui hasnae got any dope and no chance of getting any right now.'

Tim had forgotten all about that idea, but wasn't the slightest bit bothered. Kirsten was intoxication enough, from her elfin face down to her size five feet. There was that misleadingly waif-like quality that she had about her. Her accent was wonderful too; Tim had particularly enjoyed a couple of the words in her last sentence: 'hasnae' and the way that she had said 'doop' instead of dope. The day before yesterday, when they had met, she had pronounced her name, when asked for it, as 'Kosty Croo'. For somebody with a Scottish born grandmother, she was a joy to listen to.

When they were together again a few minutes later, with *If You Leave* by Orchestral Manoeuvres in the Dark playing on the radio, Kirsten asked about Rex.

'No use,' Tim replied briefly, as they rolled around on top of the yellow duvet cover. 'But I've got bad news too.'

'What?'

'I rung my mum on the way back. There's a box just when you get back into town, the end nearest to Rex's—'

'Well, I know that. But what's happened with your mum?'

'Oh, nothing, she's fine. But the mess down there – you know, the shop – it's just getting worse and worse. She wants me to go back tomorrow.'

An indecipherable look passed across Kirsten's face as she said: 'That's all right.'

'Yes, but…'

'Look, Tim… think about how long we've known each other, think about how young we are and how far apart we live, and don't pretend this is something it isn't, okay?'

She was right. How else was it going to end? Tim could hardly ask her to move to England so that they could set up home together, after just two days. Anyway, where exactly could they live? The family home with Mum and Joe? Highly likely. And what else was there to offer her? A shoe shop in its death throes and fortnightly signing on due to start any time.

They could hardly try to conduct a long distance romance. Neither of them owned a car. Tim didn't even have a driver's licence, or money to spend on the two buses each way and guesthouse fees. The idea of hitchhiking all the way from Yorkshire to the County of Angus was horrifying.

There was only one feasible outcome for their relationship and Kirsten had summed it up very neatly.

'I'll slip back down here tonight, after everyone's in bed,' she offered. 'But is there anything you wantae talk about? Now, I mean.'

'Like what?'

Them?

'Your mum. Your brother.'

'Oh... no.'

They had already ceased to exist. At least for now, for whilst Kirsten was around.

'So what shall we talk about then?'

'You think of a subject,' Tim challenged her, sliding a hand underneath her wrap around skirt and up her smooth thigh.

Kirsten considered. Something personal maybe. They had already discussed a number of general topics: music, the Chernobyl disaster, Dirty Den.

For a moment, she dallied with the idea of telling all. But no, that and this were completely separate spheres of her life. That was supposed to be a masculine way of thinking, but with everything that was going on right now, it was the only way to stay sane. Men had good ideas sometimes.

Grandad. The Somme. He had never exactly sworn her to secrecy about that; it had just seemed fairly obvious that if he wanted any other family members to know about it, he would inform them himself.

'I'll tell you a story,' she said. 'I've sometimes wanted to share it, but I never have till now, not even with people in Glasgow who've never met him. Something my grandad did in the First World War. What the hell – you aren't likely to meet him now.'

'I had two great grandfathers killed in World War One,' contributed Tim, thinking: *not likely to meet him now, meaning, I might never see her again.* Although the old man was supposed to be eighty-eight or eighty-nine.

'The more I hear about it, the more I think Grandad must be the only guy who survived it at all. Especially the Somme. He nearly lost an arm there, you know, in the first ever tank attack. Otherwise, he might've gone on to be killed at Passchendaele or one of the other battles. Scary, when you think about it; us and our dad and aunties, uncles and cousins would never've existed.'

Kirsten stopped talking momentarily and removed Tim's hand from the area of her tattoo.

'Not just now,' she said lightly. 'This is a bit serious. You can go back to checking out my special offers after.'

Tim laughed, but without real humour. There seemed so little to laugh about.

Then Kirsten began her tale and soon, despite all personal feelings and troubles, she had her chosen audience's undivided attention.

Part One
Remembering Kirsty

Gone Away, Gone Away, He Said

It's a strange experience seeing Craigston High Street again. It seems so familiar, with its pink stone buildings, yet somehow altered. Possibly though, the only thing making it appear different is my faulty memory, after so many years.

Almost everything about my life has changed since then, although one aspect of it is exactly as it was in mid-1986: my small world has fallen to pieces again.

I'm getting quite good at this. First I screw up, then I flee, albeit temporarily, to the East coast of Scotland. I'm starting to get the hang of it now.

At least I've managed, on this occasion, to create the illusion for myself that I'm finally making something happen. I'm not sure when I last felt like that.

We pass the four-storied Callum Brae guesthouse before we reach the National Express coach stop. They won't own it any more. The old grandfather will be long dead. The new people may know where they've gone though.

I've always wondered what happened to Kirsty.

I don't want to stay at Callum Brae this time, so I drop back a level from the High Street, towards the sea, where I can remember noticing other boarding houses when I was here before. As it turns out, there are only two of them; I select one with the predictable name of 'Seaview' and a man of about my own age, with receding brown hair and bluey-green eyes, shows me to a second floor room at the back, overlooking an enclosed courtyard.

I decide to take a walk along the golden beach before I make my move on Callum Brae. Exactly like last time: putting off my visit to Rex until the third day. Mind you, I did have Kirsty distracting me then.

That first meeting with her, after I'd dumped my gear in the room and was on my way out to explore the town. As I descended the stairs, I noticed the good-looking young woman talking to the good looking, but blonde, older woman who ran the place. As I nodded to them, the latter asked: 'Off to see the sights, dear?' I admitted to it and she said; 'Hang on, my daughter could show you round, couldn't you?'

Which was what Kirsty did, although she made it clear that she was not enamoured of her home town, having fairly recently returned from a stint in Glasgow. Not like me. I've been enamoured of the memory of Craigston ever since, inextricably linked, as it is, with the memory of her.

It's cold on this beach. The sea is grey and squally looking. According to my recollections, it was blue when I paddled with Kirsty and the days were warm, even if we never did get to the point of going for a swim. Still, that was July and this is May.

I make my way back up to the street; pausing only to buy a chunky Kitkat from a newsagent's, I head for Callum Brae.

Three weeks after I returned home from here in 1986, once the shop had closed and nothing seemed very worthwhile, apart from what I'd known with her, I tried ringing Kirsty. It wasn't part of the plan that I should, but I'd made a note of the phone number, so it was an option.

Her father answered. When I identified myself and asked to speak to her, there was a short silence.

'Is she no' with you?'

'No. Was she on her way down here?'

He must have thought that I sounded genuine, not to mention hopeful. He said;

'She disappeared the same day you left. We thought she might've gone with you, you being friends. She was given to just taking off.'

Disappeared. I've always found it a sinister word. The 'Disappeared Ones'. *Police are concerned about his disappearance.*

'We tried writing and the letter came back. You gave us a false address,' John Crow accused me.

I've always done that at boarding houses. A security policy. My brother broke a hotel window once, quite by accident, and if he hadn't been traceable – had he not been staying there as a member of the Sheffield United squad – he could have sneaked off without paying for it.

My brother Rex. Another of the 'Disappeared Ones'. We do at least know that he's alive and a little bit about where he's been though.

Kirsty appeared to be alive too, as she had packed up and removed a lot of her gear. Nobody, however, had witnessed her departure; she had not said goodbye or left a note.

John and I could only presume that she had returned to Glasgow. She had apparently run away before, when she was only fifteen. They hadn't known where she was until she had suddenly shown up again a few months previously, and then she had had remarkably little to say about how she had spent the intervening time.

She didn't tell me much about it either. As I knock on Callum Brae's easily recognisable blue front door (repainted by now, surely), I trawl my memory banks for any information on the subject that I might have managed to retain. She had been in Glasgow. Living in a flat. Two flatmates, was it?

A woman opens the door. To my surprise, although she is older, greyer and fatter, she is definitely Isla, Kirsty's mother.

'Do you want a room, dear?'

I love Scots accents. Having a grandmother who did not completely lose hers possibly accounts for it. There's a warmth about the way they talk up here. Isla has it. Kirsty certainly did.

'No... I'm just passing through' I say. 'You might not remember me – my name's Tim Wharton. I was friends with your daughter quite a long time ago...'

'Oh.' She peers at me, pushing her face, which is far more lined than it used to be, closer to mine. She obviously needs glasses for this kind of thing. 'Angela's no' living here now,' she informs me. 'Do you know she's married?'

'No, I mean Kirsty.'

'Oh. Oh aye, I know you. Of course. We all thought...'

'Yes. What's she up to these days? Married as well.'

A look comes into Isla's blue eyes. Despair, almost. 'Like to come in for a cup of tea?'

'That'd be lovely,' I say.

Now it's just a question of making sure that she doesn't find out I'm staying at someone else's boarding house. I could have come here again, but the idea of nights spent in Callum Brae without Kirsty seemed anticlimactic.

We pass through that often remembered hallway where I first saw her. As she leads the way down to her basement kitchen, Isla says; 'I've nothing to tell you about Kirsten. We've no' heard a word from her since she ran away again. When you were here. You've no' seen anything of her down there?'

I wish that I could tell her I have. Seventeen years is a long time for a mother and daughter to be out of touch. I've been presuming that there would have been some sort of communication between them by now.

'Someone has to know something. Someone round here. Maybe someone I know.'

But Isla makes the statement in a resigned manner, as if this is a long held belief which she may not even believe in any more.

The fact that Kirsty disappeared has really taken on a sinister ring, when you add the knowledge that nobody here has been contacted by her in all these years. That's not normal behaviour. It's about what you'd expect from my brother, but not from a member of this family. Going by the bit I know about them.

Whilst Isla makes the tea, she tells me to sit at an oak table and explains that, although she has a perfectly good kitchen in their upstairs living area, she prefers to be down here during the day, when she can find a reason to be. Business isn't good at the moment, only two guests – I feel guilty about being at Seaview – but that doesn't seem so bad if she's down here keeping busy.

'There's too many of us at it round here, now so many go abroad. We might not even be able to find a buyer when we retire, but we want to at least keep it going till then. I've two years to go and John's three, and if we can just get that far and say we've neither of us been out of work in our lives, that'll be something, won't it?'

I agree. To me, it seems unbelievable, although my father managed it too. Not that he lived to draw a pension.

'But enough about me. What about yourself?' Isla asks.

I tell her that, despite my two days and one night a week at the Crown and Anchor, I am, technically, out of work.

'That's no good. It's hard out there now though. What part of England is it?'

'The North.'

'Bad enough, I hear, but you'd maybe find it even harder up here. Devolution's no' had a good effect on the job market yet. Have you any bairns?'

'No, I'm not married.'

Isla hands me my tea, in what might be a Royal Doulton cup and saucer. Unless it's an imitation. I've worked in a couple of second hand shops, but I was never interested enough in china to learn much about it.

'How's your husband?' I enquire, as she sits down, producing a biscuit tin which I'd swear was neither in her hand nor on the table a moment ago.

'Oh, fine. Down the pub at the moment. He goes a couple of afternoons a week unless we're busy.'

From what she has already told me, I can only conclude that he goes a couple of afternoons every week.

'What about…' (what was her name again?) 'Angela? Married, you said…'

'Aye, just two years ago. I've her wedding pictures upstairs, if you'd like a look.'

What can I say? I'm not particularly interested – she was a surly looking high school kid in 1986 – but there isn't a polite way to turn the offer down.

'We'll go up when you've finished your tea then,' Isla decides, draining her own cup with almost indecent haste. I finish off the custard cream that I'm nibbling on and follow suit.

We traipse up several flights of stairs, bypassing the first floor, where I stayed last time. Isla opens the door into a living room, and the first thing I notice in it is a man of about ninety, sitting over a three bar electric fire.

He must be Kirsty's grandad. The old soldier upstairs whom I never met, but heard that spooky story about. I had taken it for granted that he would be dead by now. And he can't be ninety, because he was about that in 1986. Is he over a hundred?

'Sandy,' his daughter-in-law says, in a deliberately loud voice. 'This is… what was it again, dear? Tim – a friend of Kirsten's, who stayed here once. A while ago now.'

'Aye, well, it would be,' he replies, turning his almost completely bald head and fixing a pair of very watery eyes on me. 'She's been gone a good while. You've no' brought news of her?'

'No, sorry, I haven't seen her since then.'

'What's that?' Sandy demands, putting a hand behind his right ear and screwing his face up, which doesn't make it any more wrinkled than it already was, because that would not be possible.

'No,' Isla tells him loudly.

'Aye, well, I'm no' expecting to hear from her now.'

'I'm just showing Tim Angela's wedding pictures.'

'Aye.'

He goes back to sitting hunched in his armchair, staring into the electric fire.

'He's a bit deaf, but he's sharp enough,' Isla says quietly, once she has dug out a red vinyl covered photo album and, not unexpectedly, a pair of glasses.

'How old is he?' I ask.

'A-hundred-and-six. Looks about eighty-five, I reckon.'

He's the oldest person I've ever seen. What must it feel like, for somebody born in the 1890s, still being alive in the age of the Internet and genetic engineering?

The wedding pictures don't do much for me. The only people in them that I know are Isla, her husband and an unrecognisably grown up and pretty Angela. Sandy, presumably, was not able to attend.

I learn that the groom is Neil, the best man Paul and the bridesmaids Kay and Sharon.

'Did you meet her at all?' enquires Isla, pointing to the only black person in any of the photographs.

'I don't think so. When do you mean?'

I can't remember seeing anybody in this town whose skin wasn't somewhere in the range between my own pasty white and Kirsty's olive.

'She's Kirsten's friend Jacqui. Lovely girl – doctor's daughter. I didnae care what colour she was, I was really pleased when they got friendly. You know your daughter won't get into trouble going around with a girl like that. We paid for the wedding, so I told Angela: I'm inviting a few people I want to invite. She's a lot of time for Jacqui herself, mind. Did you no' meet her when you were here before?'

'No, but Kirsty mentioned her.'

She was hoping to buy dope through her. She used to talk about a boyfriend too; some Scottish name.

'She mentioned her a couple of times,' I expand. 'Jacqui and Duncan, I think it was.'

'Donald. Donald Shaw. They ended up married, two little girls, but it didnae last. Kirsten used to go with him too, before she ran off the first time.' The despairing look returns to her eyes. 'You hear a lot about runaways nowadays, don't you? But it was all still going on before all the fuss started, let me tell you. And homelessness. Kirsten must've been homeless, mustn't she, at least for a while? Did she say anything to you about what she did in Glasgow?'

I want to tell her something, but I have so little.

'She said she lived in a flat some of the time. I think she was doing bar work. You wouldn't be able to do that while you were living on the streets, would you?'

I'm trying not to think too hard about the possibility that that might have happened to Kirsty.

'I suppose not,' Isla agrees absently, gazing into space. Then she snaps out of it and pats my hand. 'Thanks for telling me that, dear. There's worse things than pub work, even if she wasn't really old enough to be in one. Probably lied about her age. And she must've known good people there to go back to, else why go?'

Old Sandy has nodded off by the time we finish looking at the photos. If it was me, I'd want to be up and checking him for vital signs, but Isla is probably used to this.

'He's a lovely old bloke,' she says, after I've announced that I'd better be going and she has started to lead me downstairs. 'Fit for his age – only a bit of arthritis. We'd never see him go in a home, the way so many do.

'The only complaint I've ever had about him is the way he brainwashed John into thinking we had to take on the running of this place, after his mother died. I've enjoyed it really, but we could've done without it and I hated it the first few years. John had a good job on the rigs, but Sandy had this thing that getting a guesthouse was his and Marion's dream and it should stay in the family. John's brothers and sisters didnae wantae know about it, but he was the youngest and the favourite, so Sandy brainwashed him that Callum Brae was his birthright.

'It was stupid they even still had the place by the time Marion died; he was eighty then and she was only a few years younger. Pretty sprightly though -otherwise, I suppose they'd just've ordered John home to help them years earlier. Her dying suddenly like that meant we had to sell our home and move in here; not straight away, but in the end, it was just simpler to do that. But enough about that. I've no complaints now.'

Apart from a missing daughter and business being bad. What did Isla ever do to deserve problems like those? I've always liked her and it isn't fair, I decide, as I say goodbye and promise to call in again if I'm ever back up this way.

Further along the Georgian High Street, before I turn off for my own boarding house, a lanky, grey haired man passes me. I catch a glimpse of his brown eyes, which immediately remind me of a similar pair, but it still takes me several seconds to work out that it's John Crow, on his way home from the pub.

The Whartons

It's a fresh, sunny morning and I walk along the cliffs towards Rex's. A scenic journey I well remember from last time.

He won't be there, of course, but I've decided to take another look at his cottage, anyway. His tenants may just know where he is, although that isn't very likely.

A couple of months after I was here before, my mum came up to try and talk to Rex, only to find that he'd left and rented the place out. The people didn't know where he'd gone and the estate agents whom he'd left in charge of the property were not 'at liberty to divulge.' So that was that. Personally, I couldn't believe the way that Craigston's residents were vanishing left, right and centre.

I haven't been able to get Kirsty out of my mind, either last night or this morning. It bothers me that they haven't heard from her for so long. Okay, so Rex hasn't chosen to contact us in that length of time either, but we have been in touch. Anyway, our family are strange, especially him. Kirsty and hers weren't.

Also, she did not say anything to me that indicated that she was planning to leave. It's hard to believe that she wouldn't have done.

Ideas are forming in my mind. Linda might say that there's plenty of room for them there, but then, I might say something similarly scathing back.

As I walk along the cliffs, looking down over the glittering aquamarine seascape, I keep wondering what happened to Kirsty. Nobody knows and it almost seems as if they don't expect to now, which is understandable after having to live with it for so long. Me though: I really want to know.

I'm going to find out.

If I can.

Rex's cottage is coming into view, on the far side of the road. Made of that nice pink stone. One of those poncy four-wheel drives stands in the driveway; as though this were the back of beyond and they have to ford streams whenever they go into town. What is the attraction of those things? Just being seen in one, I suppose. And why is the spare wheel so often located on the outside? If they really want it nicking, they ought to leave it lying around somewhere.

A man comes out to the vehicle, as I'm crossing the road. I stop in my tracks. Then quickly start up again, when a van appears around the nearest bend.

He's a little fatter in the face and has a salt and pepper effect in his hair now, but the bloke with the four-wheel drive is Rex.

*

We never had much in common. Understandable, considering that he was a hero and my father's favourite and I was a weirdo and my mother's. We spent virtually no time together; he was always off playing football.

The only things that mattered in our house were the Old Man's business and Rex's soccer. By the time we were maybe ten and eight, it was all mapped out for us: Rex was going to play professionally, if at all possible, and I would go into the shop as long as he wasn't available. In a lot of families, those would have been vain hopes; many schoolboy 'genius' players simply don't have the talent to make a living out of the game, and some kids tell their shopkeeper fathers to stick it, and find their own job. Not us though.

Rex had what it took. An apprenticeship with York City, then poached by Sheffield United. We'll never know if he might have made it all the way to the Manchester United/ Arsenal/ Liverpool level by the early nineties. As a midfielder, he wouldn't have been able to leave it much later than that.

Such possibilities vanished after that reckless tackle during the Crystal Palace match – not made by Rex, for a change, but on him. The sort of thing they all dread: a broken right leg that will never quite be good enough for the professional game in this country again. They told him that, eventually, and he still tried really hard to get back from it. It came at a bad time though, what with the Old Man's heart attack and the way he fell out with Mum and I. After a while, he stopped trying and crawled up here to lick his wounds.

He was crazy about the Old Man, Rex. The only person, he said, who supported him a hundred per cent and gave him the confidence to succeed. He didn't do anything like that for me.

I have to be honest, a part of me shouted: 'All right!' in that rejoicing American way, when I heard that Rex would never play again.

The Old Man must have turned in his grave. And spun a few more times when the shoe shop which he'd built up went under, run into the ground by me in less than eighteen months. I'm not especially good at selling and I'm crap at running businesses. He always said that I would be if I didn't shape up. Perhaps he'd have sold it instead of passing it on, had he not died so suddenly. That way, a shop would still exist with the legend: Arthur Wharton Shoes above its window.

That was what Rex was unable to forgive me for; it was as if he thought I was doing it on purpose. It was the reason why he didn't want to know when I took a badly needed break from the place, for my sanity's sake, and came to try and patch things up with him.

I also chose to take a holiday in Craigston because my Grandma Wharton spent the first nine years of her life here, before the family moved down our way. The Old Man never got around to bringing us here. He rarely took us anywhere for more than a day trip; he wouldn't have wanted to interfere with the business and Rex's summer football. Anyway, I don't think he was the slightest bit interested in his Scottish lineage. Not like Rex, he always loved that, hence his buying property here and continuing to pay rent in Sheffield. Just as well the Scots stuff wasn't on my mum's side of the family, or he'd have had to let it go.

My parents apparently had a lousy marriage, after the first few years. The shop, his business mates and Rex were all that the Old Man truly needed. Mum became involved with Joe a year or so before she was widowed, and the reason I know that, is that I wasn't led to believe that she met him through the funeral. Everyone else thinks she did, seeing as he's the undertaker who buried my father. Mum told me all about it a few weeks later -said she couldn't bear the idea of Rex and I not knowing the truth. I was absolutely astounded, but I wasn't able to blame her. I'd had the Old Man on my back for the whole three years that I'd been out of school and, even in death; I hadn't managed to find much sympathy to waste on him. To this day, I never have.

It was different with Rex. He told her he hated her, cut her off, repeatedly slammed the phone down on her. And on me, after a while. Then he vanished into thin air.

Grandma Wharton died when I was twenty-three. Going through her address book, to ensure that all the relevant people were informed, we found Rex listed with a Sydney address and phone number. Later, clearing the house out, we came across a studio portrait of him, smiling alongside a woman who held a baby in her arms. That was it – Mum rang the number. He grudgingly spoke to her this time. Yes, he was married and had a daughter, Gemma. He was employed as a soccer coach. He was sorry to hear about Grandma. No, he didn't want to speak to me. After a couple of letters went unanswered, Mum phoned again. He'd had the number changed.

We didn't know how much he might have told Grandma Wharton about Mum and Joe – now married – but he'd obviously found some way of persuading her to keep his whereabouts a secret. Now we had an address, but neither of us could afford to visit it. The risk of having a door shut in our faces if we did so wasn't too appealing either.

*

'Not you again,' he says, as though we last met a week ago.

'Yeah,' I reply stupidly. I'm not prepared for this, I don't know what to say.

'How did you find out I was here? And don't say the media – I'm sure they don't even remember who I was.'

'I was just up this way. Came for a walk, take a look at the house. How long you been back?'

'Five months. Expected to get away with it a bit longer than this.'

I'm not sure what to make of his manner. He hasn't extended his hand my way, or anything like that, but he isn't being as maliciously unfriendly as he was previously. Well, how could he be, after all this time?

'Were you going to get in touch?' I ask cautiously.

'I've been thinking it over. That's what you can tell her when you next talk – I'm still thinking it over and her trying to steam in now might just tip the balance the way she won't like.'

We're standing in his driveway. He leans against the car, looking at me defensively.

'You back for good or...'

'Yeah.' He hesitates, before suggesting: 'Maybe you'd like to come up here tonight?'

"Yeah, okay,' I agree, trying to sound casual. I should tell him to shove it. It isn't even him I've come looking for. Still, this is a major breakthrough. If it turns out that we still don't like each other much, I could be the one to walk away this time.

'Right then.' He peels himself off the four-wheel drive and opens its door. 'Somewhere I've got to be right now. We'll have a decent chat later.'

He doesn't offer me a lift, although he takes the road in the direction leading away from the town, so that's fair enough. I'm left in the slightly ridiculous position of standing in the driveway of his cottage waving him off.

I cross the road and begin the cliff top journey back to Craigston, wondering why I feel so excited at the prospect of spending an evening with Rex.

Meeting my niece and sister-in-law and any other children who might have come along by now will be fun, I suppose. Perhaps he's on his way to pick them up from somewhere; the cottage had a very quiet, closed up look about it.

What was his wife's name again?

Years That Slipped By Quickly

So much has happened since the last time Rex and I met. Potentially, there is a lot to tell him about. If this was a television programme, a montage of the more interesting bits would flash by in chronological order, set to music. Kirsty spending the night in my bed, kissing me off at the bus stop, then stepping through a doorway into another dimension. The almost overwhelmingly depressing sensation of being back in the shop without her, whilst it fell to pieces around me. A couple of jobs that followed, in other people's shoe shops. (I'm not even interested in bloody shoes; the only benefit I've ever derived from working with them, apart from wage packets, is that I've been left with an ability to visually assess foot sizes. An extremely useful skill, I must say. How anybody can be fetishistic about feet or shoes is beyond me.) Then there was a girlfriend who lasted about a hundred times longer than Kirsty did and was about a hundred times less interesting. Then I inherited half of Grandma Wharton's estate – my father was an only child, so it all went to Rex and I - and decided to take another gamble out on my own, but this time selling something I liked: second hand books. I got it wrong again though; went in with too little capital, spent too much of it too soon. The recession was getting under way then and books were one of the luxuries people were cutting down on. I improved on my personal best and went out of business in slightly over a year. And that was me finished in our local commercial community, a joke, for a while, amongst the other shop owners -somebody who had screwed up twice.

Except for one shop owner. I wasn't a joke to her. A matter of months before I closed, a lingerie outlet, Knickerlodeon, opened next door. Linda, its proprietor, was the absolute opposite of me. Not simply in the most obvious respect: that opening a shop is the opposite of having to close a shop, but also because of her drive and determination, her single mindedness. It's no surprise that, to this day, her business has thrived, rather than going down in a screaming heap.

By the time I found myself firmly on the receiving end of the latter experience, Linda and I were emotionally and sexually involved.

I ended up working for her, casually/on call, at least. Mainly after hours, when she needed a hand with stock. A very small component in the country's black economy.

It amuses me when politicians do an occasional rant about the evils of the black economy and pledge themselves to bringing about its eradication. They enjoy a privileged lifestyle, and to them it must, understandably, seem quite alien. For many of us though, it is simply common sense; a simplified arrangement to suit both parties, as long as it's only a temporary or sporadic thing.

I never did get back into the full-time workforce after my bookshop. Nobody warned me that everything would get so much tighter in the nineties, that I might find myself in a position where I had used up all my chances. I've had two or three part-time bar jobs, the second hand shops and various limited duration positions, generally for the minimum wage. That about covers it.

My love life has been more of a success, perhaps. Linda and I lasted eleven years, despite break up attempts, both initiated by her, when I was twenty-nine and thirty-two. At least I had my own flat, so our relationship was able to be cancelled and reinstated with the minimum of physical upheaval.

Linda did not want us to live together. She'd have been murder to share a home with, anyway. Too slovenly for my tastes. You'd never realise that she was capable of keeping a shop full of underwear so tidy, if you'd only seen the amount of it she left lying around on her bedroom floor. And the way she hangs her washing out… She doesn't even bother to colour coordinate the pegs with the items which they're holding. Always in a hurry, that's her trouble.

Our last split has proven to be more permanent. Aged thirty-seven this time, I managed to convince myself that I would turn her away if she tried to come crawling back. Five weeks went by, then she rang me up. She said she thought it only fair that I should hear it from her, that she had started going out with a man she had recently met.

Fair isn't the word that I would necessarily use. But as Linda often accused me, I do tend to look at things from my own biased viewpoint. Why not though? If I don't, who else is going to?

Jacqui

I arrive back in town feeling hungry – not to mention despondent over Linda – and make straight for a bakery.

Coming from where I normally spend my days, I don't even consciously register the colour of the woman beside me, buying an open sandwich, until the assistant says; 'See you again, Jacqui.'

Jacqui. She looks like the one in Angela Crow's wedding pictures, although her hair has grown noticeably longer since then. Putting aside my need for food, I follow her outside.

'Jacqui…'

'Yeah?'

She appears understandably puzzled.

'Do you know Kirsty Crow?'

Her eyes grow wide. They are large and brown, like Kirsty's.

'Yeah. Do you?'

'Well, I used to. Haven't seen her since the same time you last did though. Unless you've heard from her since 1986?'

'No, nothing. How did you know her? Glasgow? And how did you know me?'

I explain.

'Oh yeah,' Jacqui says, 'I think I remember her mentioning someone she'd made friends with at the guesthouse.'

'I'm trying to find out what happened to her,' I announce. Saying it out loud in front of a witness can only strengthen my resolve. Then I remember my manners. 'My name's Tim Wharton.'

'Jacqui Bassett.' We shake hands. 'Well, still Jacqui Shaw, officially, but not for much longer. Why though? Why are you looking for Kirsty now, after so long?'

I've been wondering about that myself. Why has she remained so fresh in my mind, when other people, who were important to me in different ways for longer – sometimes much longer – periods, have faded away almost completely?

And why, since Linda abdicated her key position in my life, has Kirsty come so sharply back into focus? Surely she's more than just useful therapy?

'It's the first time I've been back up here,' I say. 'I expected I'd be able to call on her family and find out how her life had turned out, maybe say hello to her. Instead, there's this big seventeen-year mystery; I could've come back up here a week later and found out what I know now. It doesn't seem right.'

Jacqui shrugs.

'Don't think I can help you.'

'Maybe if you just told me a bit about her. The sort of person she was – as you saw her. It's a start.'

Anything would be really. All I'm at right now is a standing start.

'Okay, I could do that. But I'm just on my lunch break at the moment. Got to get back to the grind soon.'

'What sort of grind do you do?'

It's only politeness; I'm not particularly interested.

'It's not bad, actually. Graphic designer. I'm one of the rare lucky ones who's doing something I enjoy.'

'Now you mention it, I think Kirsty said something about you being arty.'

'What she probably said,' grins Jacqui, 'is that it was me did that tattoo of hers, when we were fifteen. You must know the one I mean? I think she showed it to everybody.'

I'm not sure that Kirsty did tell me that, or I would have been likely to remember. It was a very good tattoo, especially if it was a homemade one done by a kid. I can't imagine asking any friend of mine to stick a needle into me, but still, what do they say – it's a dirty job, but at least your artwork lasts a lifetime.

'Tattoo?' I feign innocence. It was in a fairly personal place and I haven't a clue whether Jacqui knows the full story about Kirsty and I or not.

She smiles.

'Look, you could come round tonight, if you like, have a bit of a chat. I haven't talked properly about Kirsty in years, unless you count comforting her mother when she was in tears about her at her sister's wedding.

'Don't come till about nine though. I'll have the kids in bed by then.'

'That's all right. I'm going to my brother's first.'

'Oh, you've got a brother round these parts, have you?' she asks in a conversational manner, as she produces a pen and note pad from her handbag and writes her address down.

'I have again now. He's a bit like Kirsty – disappeared on us for years.'

There it is again. That strange feeling I get whenever I apply the word 'disappeared' to Kirsty.

'Happens in the best of families, I suppose,' suggests Jacqui. 'Mine keep in touch too much really, although I'm the only one left round here. Even my parents have gone to Aberdeen. I think I'm about the only member of my generation at school who's stayed here and had their parents leave town, instead of vice versa.'

As she walks away, it strikes me how very like Kirsty she is. Similar eyes and hair, skin only a couple of shades darker, wearing a size five trainer, which I think is about right. Equally slim and just as self-assured, with a hint of vulnerability.

Oh well, here I am again. Plenty of plans for the evening and nothing to do all afternoon.

Rex

I arrive at Rex's before seven, to give myself sufficient time there before I move on to Jacqui's. It wouldn't matter if he didn't live so far out of town.

He seems a little uncertain, but actually lets me in this time and leads the way along a hall and into a decent sized lounge, where it is immediately obvious that he was not responsible for the interior design – the carpet, curtains and furniture all go together. Even the computer appears to match; he would have to have one of those. A big window offers us an amazing view of the sea.

He suggests beer and we sit with cans of Tennent's, making conversation about nothing much. This would be a recipe for disaster on TV: two people with a history, who are awkward about being in one another's company again, having a drink or a meal together. One always ends up saying something to offend the other, who walks out, leaving their booze or food unfinished. Personally, I couldn't be as wasteful as that, no matter what he throws at me.

'About Mum and Joe...' I begin, tempting that kind of fate.

'Not now,' he says abruptly. 'I told you, I need time to think about that.'

Seventeen years wasn't long enough?

He lapses back into silence and I glance around the room for inspiration. It would be hard to miss the large framed photographs on the end wall, above the fireplace (probably just a decorative feature now, he's sure to have central heating). A boy of about nine and a girl who must be thirteen or fourteen-year-old Gemma. They are both dark and good-looking, like him. No wonder my brother has chosen to live up here: he has black hair and brown eyes, like so many of the other residents of this town with whom I have involved myself.

'Lovely kids,' I comment. 'I'd like to meet them.'

'Still in Sydney,' Rex says, glancing at me, then away. 'We split up a couple of years back. I miss them, but I just wanted to come back here.'

I feel a brief spurt of anger. I'd like to have children, and he's chosen to walk away from his access rights. Like fifty per cent of all separated fathers, according to what I've read. Trust Rex to be one of the arseholes. He hasn't even got the excuse that he had a bad role model; the Old Man was a perfect father to him, he ought to know how important a part he could play in his kids' lives – if he was in the same hemisphere.

I'd love to hear why his marriage failed. Not his side of the story though. And if I did ask, all I'd be likely to get is his 'too painful to talk about it' routine.

'What about you?' he suddenly enquires. 'Your life?'

I don't want to tell him about Linda, or that I've failed in business again. What does that leave?

'I've had quite a few jobs, but I'm only working part time at the moment, doing a few sessions at the Crown and Anchor.'

'The Crown and Anchor,' muses Rex, rather than making some quip about my implied unemployment. He must be mellowing.

I wonder how well off he is nowadays? Well enough to be living in a different world from the one I'm stuck in, anyway. He'll have looked after those investments of his. Hidden them from his wife maybe and kept them right out of their financial settlement. He was always good with money; if he'd been knocked out of the game really early on, he might've ended up running the shoe shop and it would have survived. No doubt he'd have diversified into sportswear in a big way and done exceptionally well.

'You were coaching football in Oz?' I say.

'Yeah, for a long time. Helped me get over not playing any more. Actually, I did end up as a player manager for one of the lower placed teams. I was good enough for that. Nobody you'd've heard of.'

He's right there. I don't do the pools – I've never heard of any Australian teams. There's presumably a 'Sydney United' and a 'Melbourne City', and maybe a 'Sydney Academicals' too. I gather that he was turning out for somebody more like 'Woolongong Wednesday'.

We get chatting about aunts, uncles and cousins about whom Rex has heard nothing in ages. Also our uniformly deceased grandparents. And what a great bloke the Old Man was. I let it go.

He's still got a thing about that side of the family. What he calls the 'direct line'. It sounds like something to do with British Telecom, but he's talking about the Whartons. He seems to think that there's something special about straight male descent, sons begetting sons, as though he believes that to be the main or only reason for marriage and copulation.

No, not copulation. He won't have changed that much.

Then there's the Scottish heritage, without which, we would not be sitting in this cottage, in this county. Without which, I'd never have met Kirsty.

I haven't only got the heritage itself to thank for that though, but specifically, Rex's near obsession with it. Otherwise, I might not have been interested enough to get around to coming up here.

He's back into researching all that in a big way, and proudly announces that he can trace our mob back to the first Jacobite rebellion. I don't doubt it for a minute.

On my mum's side, of course, he won't even know what any of her grandparents' Christian names were. Me, on the other hand... I'm pretty sure there was a Gladys. Every English family has a Gladys, if you just dig deep enough.

I may not be giving Rex my full attention, but at least his 'family fever' has got us talking. And drinking our second can each. Perhaps this is as good as it will ever get between us. I can't recall a time when it was a great deal better. It's enough anyway, and no doubt similar to the relationships enjoyed by a lot of adult siblings.

A little after eight, I explain that I will shortly need to dash to another appointment.

'Really? You don't know anyone up here.'

I'd forgotten about that. Since a young age, Rex has presumed that everybody else is predominantly interested in him. He would find it hard to imagine somebody chasing up here after him, as I did in '86, and still getting around to meeting other people, even if he didn't exactly monopolise my time.

'Don't tell me you've met a woman already?' is his inaccurately accurate guess.

'No. Well, yeah, but not like that. Mind you, she's the friend of someone I met here last time.'

'Hold on a minute – this is getting a bit fucking confusing. Are we talking about a bird from before or now? Need to be a bit bloody patient, wouldn't she, if she's been waiting all this time?'

So I get my turn at holding forth on a subject which is not likely to mean much to anyone else within earshot

'Are you serious?' he asks, when I've finished. 'Trying to track her down? Why?'

I'm sure that he'll have forgotten all about any three-day emotional and/or physical relationships which he has ever had. There again, none of them were with Kirsty. There is that, at least. We were all in the same town for a short time and I was the one who got off with her. Unbelievable. I'm surprised it wasn't on the news.

I want to try to explain to Rex how everything about Kirsty was exciting. Those big eyes. The sharp intellect that was often mirrored in them. Her lively sense of humour. Going to bed with her in her parents' boarding house. The tattoo, at a time when, unlike now, respectable young women were unlikely to have one. Even that story she told me.

'It was sort of like, if it was to do with her, it was interesting,' I say. 'I'm biased about anything concerning her personally, but here's an example. She was telling me about her grandad. He's an amazing old bloke; I just met him yesterday, when I visited her mother. Over a hundred. She was telling me about him killing a man on the Somme—'

'That hardly makes him unique,' Rex cuts in dryly.

'It probably does, actually,' I correct him, and explain why.

'I've met a lot of people, all round the world,' he says, when I've finished. 'So many of them seem to have secrets to tell you – often about someone else. Knowing who's telling the truth and who isn't, is the biggest problem.'

'Lots of liars out there,' I agree.

'It's a bullshitters' world.'

He ends up offering me a lift to Jacqui's. I overlook the third lager that he's started on and gratefully accept. It's a long walk, even if I do have plenty of daylight for it at this time of the year. Also, our conversation has taken a definite turn for the better. We seem to be enjoying one another's company. It's a pity that I can't stay longer, although it may be as well not to overdo it first time back.

It takes Rex a while to find Jacqui's street. He hasn't spent enough years or even months here to know Craigston inside out.

I'm a few minutes late, but the downstairs lights are still on in the end house of a tidy looking row with well cared for front gardens.

'Get in touch tomorrow or the next day, if you're not too busy with your quest,' he suggests facetiously. 'I'll just give you my mobile number.'

Trust him to have one of those, I think. But almost affectionately.

Interlude

1ˢᵗ July 1916

Glancing to one side of the sergeant, Sandy noticed Lieutenant Carter, lying face down with half of his head blown away. This was not as shocking as it might have been fifteen minutes earlier; Sandy had recently seen worse.

He caught sight of his platoon commander's Webley, a few feet in front of him, where it had dropped from the young man's lifeless hand. Acting, as he had learned to do at Loos, without a great deal of forethought, he reached out for the pistol.

He crouched there, feeling its weight, as he looked about him. He had not handled one of these before. He knew where the trigger was though. Nobody was watching.

'I thought you were supposed to be an old soldier, Crow.' Sergeant Hay breathed heavily and painfully between each shouted word. 'You're no' supposed to be stopping for bloody souvenirs. You havenae stopped to help a wounded man, I'm sure, with me being the only one.'

You're right about that, thought Sandy. Still, he could scarcely believe his ears. The bastard was unable to resist having a go at him, even now. Having him busted back down to private last month had obviously not been enough for him.

'Shut up, Hay!' he roared.

Then he turned around and shot him in the temple.

1st July 1986

Kirsten watched Sandy as he sat at the window, lost in his own thoughts. Was he dwelling on that, she wondered? The sergeant.

It had affected her a little when first he told her about it, but she could not understand why now. War was about killing, and that guy sounded to have deserved it more than the average German might have done. She had been young though, still only fifteen, when he had let her in on his secret, and it had certainly bothered her then.

It had been one of the reasons for her running away to Glasgow, albeit, a minor one. When you can't rely on any of the important people in your life, and even your grandfather turns out to be a murderer, it becomes difficult to stay.

Who would think it to look at him though? This frail old man. Kirsten had already learned never to judge by appearances, otherwise, it would have been a salutary lesson.

Another hour or so and she could get back to Tim. Tim, who now shared their secret, made an accessory seventy-years after the fact, by her. Had she done the right thing? She doubted that Sandy would think so, and was not planning to offer him the opportunity to express such an opinion.

The two of them had been left in charge of Callum Brae whilst her parents were at bingo. The old man had the knowledge about guesthouse keeping and she the young legs for running up and down stairs, if summoned.

'You're always looking at that clock,' smirked Angela, from the seat at the table where she was attending to her homework. *Different to me, at that age,* thought Kirsten, *sneaking out with Jacqui and various lads whenever I could.*

'You won't realise,' she said to her sister, 'but people who know how to tell the time do need to look at clocks now and again.'

Angela continued to smirk.

'And when the big hand is on the twelve, it's fucking time. Again.'

Sandy looked suspiciously around, but his younger granddaughter's head was down over her books. She had not spoken loudly enough for him to be sure about what he might have heard.

Kirsten half smiled. It had not been too wild a guess. She had no doubt left a reputation behind her at the school. She and at least three-dozen others, but they would have made sure that it was her whom Angela got to know about.

'Quiet tonight,' Sandy commented. 'You can slip out if you want, lass, when Angela finishes her homework.'

'Oh no she's not.' The young scholar rose swiftly to her feet. 'I've finished right now – almost finished – and I'm away to Sharon's. Kirsten gets paid round here, so she can stay.'

'I'm not getting paid for this…'

Kirsten was wasting her sweetness on the desert air. Her sister had performed a commendable disappearing act. There was hope for her yet, difficult though it was to imagine she and Sharon Rafferty getting up to anything truly interesting. Still, that was how her mother had felt about herself and Jacqui, so who could say?

The only difference with Angela was, she did her homework first. Kirsten had always found that, especially at this time of the year, when it was light for so long, a detention immediately after school, for failing to complete assignments, ate into less valuable personal time than evening studies did. As she recalled, she had employed a similar policy all the way through school: take your chances, then take your punishment, if you don't get away with it.

It could be that she was still going through life in that fashion.

She gazed fondly at her grandfather. They were alone now and it could be the last chance. It needed saying.

'Grandad…'

'Aye?'

Kirsten almost replied: 'Oh, nothing.' She checked herself.

'Love you,' she told him.

Part Two
The Real Kirsty

Back Stories

Last night, having nothing else to do, I ended up in a pub called the Commercial. That wasn't a great start, because I can't afford to spend too much on alcohol whilst I've accommodation to be paying for as well. Tonight though, I'm doing pretty well with the free stuff. Jacqui offers me a choice of white or red wine as soon as I walk in.

Her lounge is smaller than either Rex's or Isla's. Its outstanding features – for me – are a couple of seascapes hanging on the wall, done in watercolours, by her, presumably, and photographs of her daughters, which are everywhere. They are perhaps aged ten and seven and both strongly resemble the parent I am currently looking at. Another feature of the evening.

Jacqui is wearing the same nicely fitting jumper and jeans which I met her in earlier. A gas fire is burning on a low setting. Cosy.

'How's your holiday going?' she asks. 'I suppose you find it a bit cold up here? It's usually either freezing or raining or both.'

'Not much better where I live,' I tell her. 'They lionise May a lot in literature and poetry, but I can't remember many of them being too warm.'

'*Lionise.* Good word – I like it. Think I've only ever seen it in print before.

'Right. Kirsty What I've decided to do is be really honest with you. I'd be wasting your time, otherwise. Maybe I'll be wasting your time anyway, but not because I've held some little detail back that might've somehow been important. Okay?'

'Sure. I appreciate it.'

'Well, I hardly know you and you'll be away again soon, so that should make it a bit less embarrassing.' It seems as though she's still attempting to convince herself of this. I'm intrigued. 'There's only one part of it that's a bit like that, anyway, and I'm sure it'll do me good to talk about it, because it involves the way I got together with my ex-husband. When you're still together, it's not the sort of story you tell, when people ask how you met.'

More and more intriguing.

'This is intriguing,' I comment. 'Doesn't sound as if you're going to bore me.'

'I'm not a boring person. Kirsty was the exact opposite of what that word means.' Jacqui smiles. 'You were joking before, weren't you, pretending you didn't know about that tattoo I did for her?'

'Well...' I can't resist teasing her further. 'You seem to think I was.'

'Look, I don't mean to pry, but, I mean, to come looking for her again after so long doesn't make it sound like you were just platonic. Kirsty was never the most platonic of girls, anyway.'

'I thought she was your friend,' I mildly protest, partly in order to postpone giving her an answer.

'She was. I didn't disapprove of her. Well, only in the early days, like most of our primary school teachers used to, because she was a bit of a tomboy and a bit cheeky and a bit mischievous and a bit lazy – a bit of everything girls weren't supposed to be. She never really lost most of that. But those of us who knew how lovely she was, didn't mind, did we?'

'No,' I agree, perhaps confirming Jacqui's suspicions.

'I didn't start getting friendly with her till high school,' she continues, 'but we were in the same class for the second half of primary. I don't know how she got on before that, but by the time I started noticing her, she was the sort of kid who was in trouble a lot. Especially in Mrs Mitchell's class. She didn't take shit from anyone. She'd march kids outside and smack them or give them the strap, boys mainly, apart from Kirsty. She was a real hard woman. Kirsty and her had a major personality clash from the word go. She didn't seem to realise that hitting Kirsty just made her more defiant. She was a brilliant teacher though, otherwise, and it was all so unnecessary – she only had to raise her voice, most of the time. I got on fine with her; I was never touched at school, but I was terrified of her, I always felt sort of under threat. Which is a pity, when all I really wanted to do was learn because I was interested, not because I was scared.

'Kirsty was totally different. She always strolled out of the room with Mrs Mitchell and back in again, looking like she couldn't give a toss.'

This is certainly a side of Kirsty's life about which I knew nothing, although the idea that she was a free spirit and cool in the face of adversity seems completely in character. Now I think about it, I'm not sure that she said very much about her childhood.

'There was a reason, of course,' elaborates Jacqui. 'Kirsty had to behave herself at home; she told me once that school was where she relaxed, because the worst she could get there was a strapping.

'She must have had a normal home life at first, I suppose, but then her grandmother died and her dad left the oil rigs and moved them all in to help run the guest house. Her mother hated it. Turned to the bottle, basically. And stopped being a decent mother. Angela was more of a wimp, so she avoided the brunt of it, but Kirsty… she told me at high school that when she annoyed Isla and she was pissed, she used to beat her up.'

'What?'

I've always dreaded this. All those people on the news doing terrible things – people somebody else knows and likes. Isla has played a very small role in my life, but I still don't want to believe that it's finally happened to me: someone I thought of as a good person turning out to be a monster.

'I don't know the fine details,' Jacqui says. 'She never came to school with black eyes; she never said she actually got punched or kicked. What she did talk about was being backhanded across the face and having chunks of her hair pulled out and being pushed against walls and thrown across her room.'

'God, this is terrible!'

'Try hearing about it in your teens. And you know what? Kirsty's dad never made a serious effort to stop it. She blamed him just as much. There was only her grandad tried to help them and he got told to keep out of it.

'More wine?'

I feel that I need it.

'Impossible to understand a man like that,' I say. 'John Crow, I mean. Just letting his own daughters…'

'Get the shit beaten out of them,' supplies Jacqui, shaking her head as she pours the Riesling.

'This wasn't still going on when I was up here, staying there, was it?' I ask.

'Oh no. It was one of the main reasons Kirsty ran away when she was fifteen, going on sixteen. Believe it or not, Isla managed to get herself right off the booze while she was gone. AA, and all the rest of it, maybe knowing why her daughter had taken off shocked her into it. Even stopped bloody smoking. Kirsty couldn't credit it when she got back and found this squeaky clean new mother. And she said the old cow never even mentioned what she'd done to her – like it just never happened. Not that she'd've put up with it if she'd tried apologising. Said she'd have smacked her one for that as quickly as she would if she'd raised her hand to her.'

'This is unbelievable, Jacqui. I've always really liked Isla.'

'I know,' she empathises. 'I still sort of do. She invited me to Angela's wedding. She always treated me like the sun shone out of my arse when we were kids. I knew it was partly because my dad's a doctor, and I hated her for a bit after Kirsty told me how violent she was, but I still had to be polite and... well, she did make the effort to change herself, I suppose. Bad timing though, with Kirsty coming back from Glasgow feeling ready to hit back at last. She'd've deserved that.'

'Do you know much about her time in Glasgow? She only told me odds and ends.'

'No, she didn't seem to want to go into details about it,' replies Jacqui. 'Think she had to live rough at first. July, August time, luckily. Then she got into a squat, real nice people, she said. There was something about working in a nightclub, but she said that had led her into trouble and that someone was out to get her, that was what made her come back here all of a sudden. She'd have stayed there if things had gone right. But that was all she'd say about it.'

'Someone was out to get her?'

Add that to the new light that has been shed upon her own mother's relationship with her and 'disappeared' definitely has that sinister ring about it again.

'It's what she said. She could always be a bit melodramatic though, when we were kids. And it was typical of her to only tell half a story. She never, ever lied though.'

That's good. A lot of people do that, as Rex mentioned earlier. Simply not being told things is far preferable. Especially when the person concerned was under no obligation to have told you them in the first place.

'And you haven't heard from her once since she left the second time?' I double check.

'Honestly, no. I'd've kept it from her family if she'd asked me to, but no, she hasn't been in touch. We weren't really as close by then, I suppose. Although it was great to see her again, same as it still would be now. She was around for a few months, then suddenly away again. The family thought she'd gone off with you.'

If only she had. If only I'd felt able to make the offer. She might have jumped at the chance for all I know, with somebody after her, like that.

It could have meant the difference between life and death.

'Weren't you worried when you found out she wasn't with me?' I ask, 'that maybe the person who was after her had caught up with her?'

'It did cross my mind,' Jacqui admits. 'But she hadn't made it sound as serious as that. More like she'd've been risking a hiding if she'd stayed in Glasgow. And she had every reason not to want another of those, although that makes it sound as though she was frightened of violence and she certainly wasn't. She got too used to it.

'Hey, that reminds me – you know I was telling you about Mrs Mitchell? Well, she got her back in the end. After she'd been back a while, she was round at my house one day when my mother was out, smoking a bit of dope, and I remembered there'd been a write up in the paper about Mrs Mitchell, now she was the head-teacher at our old school. She still is. It was all about how she'd banned corporal punishment, which I thought was a bit ironic, and not one word said in the interview about how she'd used to use it quite a lot, just her opinion that it was ineffective. I managed to dig it out for Kirsty and she reacted like I expected -

even threatened to go round and have a word with her about it. She'd never have bothered, but we were in town a few days later and ran right into Mrs Mitchell. She had another woman with her – you could tell she was a teacher too – and Kirsty just couldn't resist it. "Hello, Mrs Mitchell," she said. "Kirsty Crow". She was all friendly and said what a fine young woman Kirsty had grown into, and she started gushing to the other woman about what an ace teacher Mrs Mitchell was. (I was edging away by this time, getting very worried about what she might be going to do.) "Oh, I know," the woman said. "I've seen her in action." "Not the way I have," said Kirsty. "She was one of those teachers who worked out what each child needed and saw that they got it." The woman said that didn't surprise her and Kirsty said; "in my case, I was a naughty little girl and what I needed was my bottom smacking. Mrs Mitchell saw that I got it – and a few whacks across the hand, as well. It was actually a very effective punishment, Mrs Mitchell, thank you very much, and I'm just wondering whether to get in touch with the paper and tell them that. Anyway, I better not hold you up." And off she went, leaving this shocked sort of silence behind her.'

'Wow!' I say. 'That sounds impressive.'

'Oh, she could be. We went to a party once where she pretended to be Italian all night. Even when she was off snogging, apparently. Maybe she had to though, if that was the reason she managed to get that snog. He was gorgeous.'

'So was she,' I remind Jacqui. 'And she already had a lovely accent.'

'Not round here, it's not. But you're right: Kirsty didn't need to put on silly voices to interest boys, not every other single time I saw her pull the one she was after.

'That was one of the best things I ever saw her do though, getting her own back on Mrs Mitchell like that, straight off the cuff. Even left her worrying about whether she was really going to go to the paper, I should think.'

I'm beginning to understand now why I have always thought Kirsty so special. She quite simply was.

I notice the pictures of Jacqui's daughters again.

'What are your girls called?'

'Carol and Natalie.' Her face softens, but only temporarily. 'They deserve a lot better than they've had recently from Don, my ex, running off to Dundee with his girlfriend and just about forgetting they exist.'

Another of those fathers.

'From what I can see, that makes him the loser.'

I'm careful to stare at the photographs as I say it, and not towards her.

'That's how we might look at it, but him... well, they're not the same sex or colour as him, are they, so why would he care? I'm sure he didn't feel like a loser – dumping his boring thirty-two-year-old wife for a twenty-four-year-old.'

I pull a sympathetic face, unsure as to what I ought to say. Then the ideal line occurs to me.

'Someone just broke up with me after eleven years.'

Jacqui shakes her head.

'Bet that feels like shit too. Him and me were married nine years. Together nearly sixteen.

'You could give up on human beings, couldn't you, the way a lot of them treat the ones they're supposed to care about? Although I doubt many of us are perfect in that department. Which brings me to the bit I haven't told you yet.'

'The embarrassing part?'

'That depends how you look at it too. Kirsty could probably tell the story without feeling embarrassed, the Kirsty I used to know. Although she's probably changed as much as the rest of us, by now.'

If she's alive. If someone didn't kill her shortly after the two of us last saw her. Not one word in seventeen years. So, her parents were arseholes and she hadn't talked as though she liked her sister much. But what about Jacqui? What about old Sandy? She seemed to hold him in high esteem, as I recall, her battle scarred grandfather who had killed soldiers on both sides. Surely she would have contacted the people who mattered to her, eventually.

'How would you describe Kirsty?' Jacqui demands. 'Sexually, I mean?'

'Ah... well...'

'Sorry, I don't mean to embarrass you. You could tell me to

piss off if I'm being too personal – although as you're in my house and this is all part of me trying to be helpful, I wouldn't recommend it.'

She says the second sentence with her twinkly-eyed smile in place; a phenomenon which I'm starting to enjoy.

How to reply to her though? I don't want to admit that I once felt like crawling right up inside Kirsty, because she made me feel so happy and safe, unlike any other aspect of my life at that time. That wouldn't really be answering the question, anyway.

Nor would telling Jacqui that Kirsty has come to represent my youth. I sometimes feel as though she was the only true moment of it that I ever experienced, post-childhood at least, what with having the responsibility of the shop pushed onto me so young. Now that I seem to have entered a premature middle age, brought on, I think, by the debilitating arguments that Linda and I were having during our last months together, but which my pacific single lifestyle has not rid me of, the romantic – as opposed to purely sexual – memory of Kirsty has more of a nostalgic glow about it than ever.

'She seemed pretty broad-minded,' I venture at last. 'Probably hadn't quite taken the safe sex message on board.'

'Early days for HIV, anyway,' says Jacqui. 'We were only just starting to listen to the announcements, and then mainly because people were actually saying 'condom' on telly, which seemed so unbelievable.

'But what you said sums her up perfectly. With sex, Kirsty was always after something different and new. She sometimes confused "new" with "new boyfriend", but every time we heard about some sexual practice we didn't know about, she was usually interested. Apart from totally disgusting things, especially anything involving violence, because she already knew that was shit.

'There was this night, just before she ran off. It'll really put it in a nutshell for you. We'd organised for me to do her that tattoo, bought the ink and everything. Afterwards, we were meeting Don, who was her boyfriend then.' She gives a slightly sheepish grin and continues. 'I'd just broken up with somebody, so we were meeting Don's mate Pete too, who I was sort of being fixed up with.

'Kirsty and I had a joint behind some garages, as a painkiller for her, then we went to my bedroom and she lay on my bed with her skirt up and I tattooed that poppy on her inner thigh. I think I was about as excited about doing it as she was about getting it.'

Personally, I was excited about seeing it.

'She needed to have it somewhere Isla wouldn't accidentally get to see it and knock her head off,' Jacqui explains. 'Bit of a challenge, but I made a good job of it, if I say so myself. The only tattoo I've ever done in my life. Never fancied giving myself one, I'm a wimp about anything painful. That must've been all in a day's work for Kirsty. Maybe she liked the idea of volunteering for pain instead of having it thrust on her. Not that she ever said that. Still, if she's had kids yet, I bet she found childbirth a bloody sight easier than I did.

'After that, we went to meet the lads. It was summer, so my mum didn't mind me going out for a walk with Kirsty, as I told her. About halfway there, she asked if I wanted to try something a bit different. I asked what she meant and she said; "Would you like a go on my boyfriend?" "What?" I said and she said; "Swap. You go with Don and I'll go with Pete. And don't pretend you don't fancy him, because I've seen you sneaking looks at each other." Well, that was true, so I told her I'd do it, but asked, what if they didn't want to? Kirsty laughed at the very idea and told me her and Don had talked about doing something like this with me, and that if Pete turned her down, she could deal with it. Like she thought for a moment that any boy would ever do that to her.'

'She never mentioned any of this to me,' I say.

It seems now that she didn't mention very much at all.

'I'm sure she'd done lots more interesting stuff in Glasgow by the time you met her. Unlike me – it's about the only really wild thing I ever did and even then, it ended up in marriage, so how wild is that? But Kirsty talked me into it easily enough; I certainly did fancy Don and who could turn down an opportunity like that? And she was right – the lads went for it like a shot. She soon got them in the right mood. We met them and got into Don's car, me in the front beside him and her in the back next to Pete. "Hey, guys," she says (she was always saying "guys" like she was from

America or Glasgow or something), "wanner see the fucking brilliant tattoo Jacqui just did me?" And she pulls her skirt up and shows it, along with her legs and knickers and everything."

I vividly recollect something similar in my room at Callum Brae. Kirsty standing in front of me like a lingerie model posing for the camera, showing off Jacqui's artwork. Except that models, even when they're wearing underwear almost too skimpy for the human eye to detect, never seem to have what you might call a hair out of place. Wild dark curls were exploding out of Kirsty's panties in three different directions…

'Then she said; "change of plan tonight, guys," and started snogging Pete.' Jacqui drags me out of my not especially unpleasant flashback and returns me to her not so far unpleasant one. 'Don turned the ignition on and put his hand on my leg, in a nervous way as we drove.

'That was how it stayed: them quite a few steps ahead of us. By the time we got to this park-up spot along the cliffs, we were touching each other, but they were horizontal. We had our first kiss, with them heavy breathing in the back, then I had to nip out for a wee.

'It was still light and when I came back, I could clearly see Kirsty's bum going up and down through the side window. I was mesmerised for a moment by the sight of her sphincter going in and out, for any other park up couples who might've come along to see too, if any had. I think that's when I realised how different we really were.'

I don't think I ever saw Kirsty's sphincter. I would imagine it to have been a nice hot pink colour. Linda's is grey.

'Was she a bit of an exhibitionist?' I ask.

'Not in the slightest. God, can you imagine Kirsty with those sorts of tendencies? She'd've been streaking down the High Street in a mask by the time she was fourteen, if that sort of stuff turned her on. No, the thing with her is, if she wanted to do something enough, she'd just do it, if there was half a chance she might get away with it. And if the risk was that she might be caught bending – literally, almost, that time in the back of the car – well, the other thing about Kirsty was, she knew that what she had was very nice, so she wouldn't have felt like she had to run off and hide in a convent afterwards.'

'Has anybody ever thought about checking round the local convents for her?'

It's an idea. An idea which causes Jacqui to shriek far too loudly, considering that she has children in bed upstairs.

'I caught Kirsty's eye as I got back in the car,' she eventually continues. 'She winked at me and a bit after that, it became obvious that things on the back seat were reaching a conclusion. Then she suddenly shouted; "how's it going in front?" That killed it for us; I'm sure she'd've enjoyed watching her best friend and boyfriend making out, but we weren't into that. We all smoked a bit of dope, then drove back to town and they dropped us girls off.

'Don rings me the next day. Says he wants to be with me properly, on our own. I say, "what about Kirsty?" and he says he's breaking up with her and wants to go out with me instead.'

Jacqui looks me straight in the eye.

'You can guess the rest, can't you? I made myself believe it was okay to take him off her, because she couldn't possibly be serious about him, after what she'd done with Pete. She didn't see it that way. Went on at me about how much she wanted Don and how all she'd done was been generous and encouraged us to have a bit of fun and this is what we did to her. I said; "come on, Kirsty, it was just as much for your own benefit. Why don't you give it a try with Pete, the way Don and I are?" "I don't want that with him," she said. "I just thought it would be a laugh to swap and okay, yeah, I wanted to have a proper, all the way one night stand; I'd never quite had one before. But I don't want to see him again." I told her she wanted to have her cake and eat it and she said; "Course I fucking do, who doesn't? And don't preach at me or I'll shove your head into that wall."

'She ran off a week or two later, so that was partly my fault. When she came back though, she was really friendly to Don and I, like there'd never been a problem. We weren't as close as we had been, but maybe that would've happened anyway.'

Jacqui leans back in her chair, and I can't help admiring the shape of her jumper. Even with my head whirling from all that she has told me, as well as the possibility that we may be discussing somebody who is now an undiscovered corpse, I am unable to avoid being attracted to this frank, forthright and beautiful woman.

'That's about it,' she announces. 'Some sort of portrait of Kirsty for you. Hope I didn't forget to mention how kind and supportive she could be and what a sweetie she was. Not one useful piece of information to help you find her, but maybe I'd've had a go myself if I'd thought I knew something.'

'Thanks, Jacqui,' I say.

'Did you love her?' she unexpectedly asks.

'No, we weren't together long enough.'

That's always seemed like yet another of the good things about Kirsty. I suspect that we might not have worked out in the long run, but as it was, we didn't have to discover that the hard way.

'Just leaves me then. I loved her, in that closer-than-sisters, teenage-girl way. Even if I was so shitty to her with Don. Still, I can't even regret that really, because I'd never have had Carol and Natalie if I hadn't been prepared to do that. That more than makes up for losing him and her.'

How much is justifiable, I wonder, if one gets a child or two out of it?

'You won't be offended if I turn you out now, will you?' asks Jacqui. 'Work and school in the morning.'

'Did you do the paintings?' I enquire, at the front door.

'Yes.'

'They're good.'

'Thanks. They're okay. Why don't you get in touch again before you go? Come to dinner or something; see, it's true – flattery gets you everywhere. Where you staying?'

'The Seaview.'

As I wander back to that establishment, through the narrow streets, I mull over my suspicions. There wouldn't have been any point in sharing them with Jacqui; she didn't take the possibility of Kirsty's having been killed by her Glasgow enemy seriously. I doubt that she would react any differently if I floated the idea of Isla. She's spent so long thinking of her as somebody who duffed up her daughters, but left them in one piece, that I can't imagine her contemplating a time when she might have gone too far.

Then there's the teacher. An outside chance, but she must

have felt threatened when Kirsty called her bluff about going to the newspaper. I can just hear Jacqui laughing at that though: 'Away! She was handy with a tawse, no' a switchblade.' Not that she does lapse into dialect like that. And where did I pick up the word 'tawse'? I must bring it out to impress her, next time.

I suddenly realise that I'm passing Callum Brae. I gaze up at it. It doesn't look any different, but it should, considering that I know now about the sickening events which have taken place in there.

It won't worry me in the slightest if she learns that I'm staying at Seaview.

The Disappeared One

After I've been served a full English breakfast in a Scottish boarding house, I ask directions of its female co-owner, referred to by her husband as Jess, to the Craigston library. I spend a little time there looking Kirsty up in the appropriate telephone books for: Glasgow, Edinburgh, Dundee and Aberdeen. None of the K. Crows that I find have the correct middle initial, I. for Isla.

The problem is that, if she's in a phone book anywhere, she quite possibly has a different surname by now.

My main plan this morning is to go for a decent walk in the country and mull everything over. It's a brisk sort of day, sunny with minimal warmth, and there's a village called Eskmill a few miles away which might be worth a look. If it isn't though, I won't know that until I'm there looking at it.

What I need to do before starting on that is to ring home. Who, is the only question. I had been planning to speak to my mum about now, but I don't want to do that without mentioning Rex, and he's right, she would contact him immediately and risk blowing everything.

I consider ringing Linda, but decide against it. I wish I knew how I really feel about her. I still love her, and there are so many bad things about us being apart, not the least of which is that I have nobody to pick the pimples on my back any more. I'm tending to agree with her though: we didn't have much of a future. I feel more optimistic than usual about that today. My future. I have to admit that spending last night in Jacqui's company has a bearing on this.

I told Bob and Mandy at the Crown and Anchor that I'd let them know how long I was going to be up here, so it may be time for me to do that.

'Oh, 'ello, Tim,' Mandy says anxiously. 'God, I wish you 'adn't rung.'

'Charming! That's more the sort of abuse I'd expect from

Bob.'

'Perhaps you'd be better talking about this with 'im. Oh, but no, 'e'd just blurt it out, dead tactless.'

I get it. They've discovered that the pub functions perfectly well with one less member of the part-time staff.

'If there's something you want to tell me, Mandy...'

'Your Linda's been seen around with a feller,' she blurts out, dead tactless. 'Tom Jarvis saw 'em coming out of the Taj Mahal on 'is way 'ere last night. I won't tell you exactly what 'e said, but—'

'It's all right, Mandy, I already know. Linda and I are just friends now, remember.'

Sort of friends.

'Oh. That's great. I was worried we'd 'ave to be the ones to tell you.'

Poor old Mandy. It's not a task she'd have relished.

She passes me on to Bob – not without putting him in the picture first –and he's soon booming at me in a more exaggeratedly Yorkshire accent than there is any need for. It's something which he and many of our regulars and men all over the county do almost automatically, upon entering licensed premises.

'You stopping up there then or what, you idle bugger?'

This telephone box is within sight of the deserted beach and it's an appealing thought. I gaze idly out across the sands. They tell me that half of what was once there has been washed out to sea in recent years, but it's still a beautiful sight. This and the pink stone buildings and Jacqui and not giving up on Kirsty are reasons enough to keep me up here for as long as possible.

'I'll be a few more days yet. My br—'

I stop myself in time. Bob knows my mum, so mentioning my brother is not the best idea.

'Oh aye? A few nice looking lasses up there then, are there? 'oo'd've thought it in Scotland? I'll be on next train up.'

'Struggling by okay without me, are you?' I dare to ask.

'Struggling by! Place is running like bloody clockwork. Buggered if I can see why we bother employing you.'

★

Eskmill is a pleasant village, with a pleasant pub where I enjoy a couple of pints of Younger's and steak and kidney pie. They're all pleasant too.

The walk here took me through horticultural countryside, which, whilst it would not qualify as an area of outstanding natural beauty, was still a good place to be on a sunny day. Crap in the rain or snow though, I should think.

After my meal and drinks, I relax with a chunky Kitkat on a seat in the village green, which provides me with a view of a row of cottages, each of which still has an old-fashioned, green painted water pump standing outside it.

As I'm admiring them, I think about Kirsty yet again.

I hate the idea that she might be just a pile of bones. Are there any statistics, I wonder, on missing persons? How many eventually turn up alive and how many are proven or strongly presumed to be dead. And how many remain forever unaccounted for, leaving friends and relations guessing.

What are my chances of getting the police interested in her case, at this stage? Where they even brought into the picture in 1986? With people like Isla and John Crow, who can say?

There are so many factors in favour of Kirsty having been murdered. Someone in Glasgow was out to get her; how hard can it be to track somebody to where the bosom of their family live? And it could be the family who caused the problem.

The worst aspect of all this is that it's like those allegations of child abuse against Woody Allen and Michael Jackson. I'll probably never know the truth. Even if she is still on the planet, how can I really expect to find her? I'll be yet another who is going to be left guessing.

Sandy is the problem. Surely she wouldn't have let him wonder for years whether she was dead or alive? Which is why it's so difficult to imagine her being alive.

Death

The walk back is tiring. I don't come up with any answers.

Arriving in Craigston late in the afternoon, I'm dragging myself through the commercial end of the High Street, when I hear my name being called.

'I've been trying to get hold of you,' cries Jacqui, pounding up behind me. 'I've left a message at Seaview and everything. Then I just look out the window and there you are.'

'Why?'

I'm flattered that she wants to speak to me so desperately.

'Do you not know?'

'Know what?'

There's something about the way she says it. This is important.

'Is it Kirsty?' I demand.

A woman's skeleton has been discovered nearby.

She's back in town.

Someone has confessed to her murder.

A woman's skeleton has been discovered nearby.

'There's been a double murder up at Callum Brae.'

Jacqui watches me intently as she says this. Then her face relaxes, appearing relieved, almost.

'What? A couple of guests?' I ask in shock. I should have said 'all the guests' I suppose, to be accurate.

'Isla and her father-in-law.'

'Are you serious?'

'Yes. I wouldn't joke about this shit.'

'But... I only saw them the day before yesterday. He's a hundred-and-six. He's lived across three centuries.'

Why is that important?

'Unbelievable, isn't it?' Jacqui sighs.

'Was it John Crow?'

It is usually the husband, isn't it? Nothing much would

surprise me now, with that family. But patricide?

'They're still investigating, of course, but they're saying he was at the Blacksmith's Arms when it happened.'

One of his afternoons at the pub.

'They say he spends most of the day there sometimes,' continues Jacqui. 'I think it's supposed to have happened early this afternoon. John went home and the police were already there; one of the guests had come back and found the bodies. I couldn't really imagine John doing anything like that.'

'I didn't really get to know him,' I admit. 'He seemed like a quiet sort of bloke. Not the sort you'd expect anything like that from.'

'Horrible, isn't it?'

It is. I even feel sick about Isla. A woman whose company I was enjoying forty-eight hours ago.

Jacqui allows herself a tight smile.

'I wanted to be sure,' she tells me. 'I had to know. I tell you about her beating Kirsty up and someone kills her the next day. I haven't been able to think straight. But I saw your reaction, how shocked you were. You're not an actor. It was probably a burglary, like they're saying.'

She suspected me.

Still, who can blame her, under those circumstances?

'How did they die?'

'Don't know. I'm sure we'll be finding out.

'You do understand, don't you? I couldn't imagine you doing something like that, that's why I didn't go straight to the police. I wanted to check you out myself first. In a public place, of course.'

'That's all right,' I assure her.

'It's with not knowing you very well,' she continues to explain. 'It's hard to know what people are capable of, isn't it? Look at Isla – who'd've thought she'd do what she used to do?

'Why don't you come for dinner tonight?'

'To your house?'

'Leave it till around half-past six. The girls stay with our friend, next-door-but-one, 'til I get in, so I don't even have them to prepare the food before I finish work. Which I'd better get back to right now. See you later.'

'Lovely, thanks,' I say. 'See you then.'
Dinner with a woman who thought I was a murderer?

★

I arrive back at Seaview. My red haired landlady – if that's the correct term for somebody so much younger than the average boarding house keeper – is standing behind her small reception desk.

'Oh, hello,' she greets me. 'A Jacqui Bassett has left a message for you to phone her. I've her number here, for you.'

'That's okay, thanks, I've just run into her.'

'Oh, good,' she says. Then, after a moment's hesitation: 'I know her, by the way. Jacqui.'

'Do you?'

'A little bit. Her dad used to be my doctor. And we were friends with two sisters. Jacqui was a couple of years ahead of Angie and me at school.'

Everyone seems to know everyone around here.

'Angie Crow, right?' I say. 'You heard the news about her mother and grandfather?'

'My God, the word's got around fast on that.'

'Actually, it's what Jacqui wanted to talk to me about. I knew them too.'

'Did you?'

'Not that well,' I say quickly. 'It's me who should be offering you condolences.'

A hard look comes into Jess's blue eyes.

'No need for that. I hardly knew the grandfather and I couldn't stand the mother.'

'Oh, I see.'

'She used to smack Angie around, you know. Get drunk and knock both her daughters about. The older one was really naughty, especially when she got in her teens – boys and running away and that sort of thing, but she still didnae deserve that, and Angie was a real good girl. Never made much difference though.

'I found out about it while we were still at school and I've been refusing to speak to the woman just about ever since. She wasnae very pleased when Pete and me bought this place, became her opposition. Angie got married around then and she wasnae allowed to invite us to the wedding. That mother of hers was a real bitch and you're better knowing the truth about her.'

'Jess…' a voice reproaches her from the nether regions somewhere behind her.

'I'll no' be a hypocrite because she's dead, Pete.'

It's a definite feeling of déjà vu: the old friend of a Crow daughter openly airing her views on the family, as though she has known me all her life. The late Isla seems to inspire such conversations.

'I feel sorry for Angie's grandfather,' announces Jess. 'He used to try and stop her, when she was out of control, but he was an old man, even back then. Fancy being murdered at that age. He was going on for a hundred, I think. He'd've been getting a telegram from the Queen, but for this.'

'He was a hundred-and-six, actually.'

She glances at me suspiciously.

'Thought you only knew them a bit?'

'Well, to be honest with you, I used to be quite friendly with Kirsty. She seemed pretty close to her grandfather.'

'Oh, you're right there. Angie always reckoned she was his favourite. And her dad's, much good that did her. She could be quite bitter about it.'

I feel an immediate empathy with Kirsty's sister. I can remember what it was like to know, without needing to be told, that the Old Man liked Rex better.

'It isn't always easy being a younger sibling,' I say. 'Especially if the novelty never quite wears off the older one, with a parent or grandparent.'

'Don't ask me, I'm an only child. I used to be glad of it, hearing what Angie had to say. Kirsten was prettier and more outgoing, and if that got her more bruises, it got her more boyfriends too. They were always teasing Angie about her sister at the high school. I won fifty pee off one of the others once, betting her someone would make Angie cry again by the end of the week, giving her a hard time about Kirsten and the boys. Nobody would take that bet again afterwards, or I'd've made more.'

'Don't think I'd like a friend like you.'

Jess grins. 'I was always a bit of a businesswoman.'

'It's been good talking to you,' I tell her. 'Interesting. I'm actually trying to find out what happened to Kirsty. Where she disappeared to.'

'You'll have work cut out there. Cannae blame her though. Who'd want parents like hers in their life, once they had a choice? And it's done Angie good, getting out from under her shadow.'

As I'm climbing the stairs, I hear Pete, the husband, tucked away somewhere on the far side of a brown curtain behind the desk, saying; 'You're just lucky. You could've caused offence there and cost us business.'

Chilli, Wine and Suspicions

'What's England like?' asks Natalie.

'You've been there,' Carol reminds her.

'I cannae remember it.'

'Can't,' corrects Carol.

'It's quite like here really,' I answer lamely. 'Except that…'

'The beer's no good,' suggests Natalie helpfully, 'That's what my dad says.'

Carol rolls her eyes. Jacqui and I laugh. They're a great couple of girls, these two. Like their mother, they have strong personalities, especially Carol, and are fun to share a table and chilli con carne with.

'Do you like it here?'

'Visitors don't want a thousand questions, Natalie.'

'That's all right, Carol,' I say. 'Yes, I do like it here, Natalie. It's a lovely part of the country. My brother likes it so much, he's bought a cottage just outside town.'

'Do you agree with the Scottish Nationalists?'

'Yeah, I do really. I can see their point.'

'That's good,' Natalie grins at me. 'Mum and Carol are Scottish Nationalists. I don't really mind. My dad thinks it's all a load of rubbish. My grandma and grandad don't agree with it—'

'Shut up about him,' snaps Carol. '

'What? Grandad?'

'No, Dad. He's the one who's a load of rubbish.'

'It's all right, Carol,' says Jacqui calmly. 'She's allowed to talk about him.'

'I never liked my dad much either,' I tell Carol quietly, after dinner, when the others are momentarily out of earshot.

'You're lucky,' she scowls. 'I wish I'd never liked mine.'

She's nine, but seems older, and Natalie's six. We all end up playing cards until it's time for them to go to bed. When I was their age, it was Snap, Happy Families or Donkey, for Rex and I, but these girls are into Bridge and have to teach me as we go along. I have learnt it before, but I can't retain details such as rules of games for longer than about five minutes after I stop playing.

'It must seem hard to believe,' Jacqui says, pouring the wine, 'but those two up there keep me sane.'

'Not hard at all,' I assure her. 'If I had kids, I'd probably be sane by now.'

She laughs. Briefly.

'Thanks for not saying anything about the murders in front of them. They'll have to know soon, but not yet.'

'How do you feel?' I ask.

'With my hands.'

'What? Oh, right, yeah, I get it. Very good.'

'It's not; it's nearly as bad as the joke you just made. It was one of my ex-husband's. What does that tell you about him?'

'That he had a sense of humour?'

'Yes, and that he's fairly intelligent, considering,' she admits grudgingly. 'And also, that he hardly ever wanted to talk about his feelings, when you consider how often he said that when I was genuinely asking him how he felt.'

'I was genuinely asking you too.'

'I know,' Jacqui lapses into thought for a few seconds. She is in a black jumper and black trousers tonight. They look amazing on her.

'I'm upset about Isla and her father-in-law,' she replies at last, 'but maybe not as much as I'd expect to be. I hadn't seen him for quite a few years; he hardly leaves the top floor of Callum Brae now. Hardly left, I mean. Probably couldn't get down the stairs any more. And I just don't know about Isla. I've always been confused about her. I ought to think it serves her right, but like I told you, I still liked her really.'

This reminds me of Jess, with her less equivocal attitude on the same subject, and I tell Jacqui about our conversation.

'Oh, Jessica, yeah, I know her, didn't realise that's who I was speaking to on the phone. I did hear she'd bought a guesthouse, but I didn't know which one. One of those people you say "hello" to in the street, but don't stop to chat, if you know what I mean. Tell you who her husband is though–'

'I know him. Pete.'

'Yeah, Pete MacCallum' smirks Jacqui. 'The same Pete who was at it with Kirsty on the back seat while Don and I were starting our courtship in the front.'

I'm staying under the roof of a man who once used the lovely Kirsty for casual sex? Although, it was the lovely Kirsty's idea, and she was definitely using him.

'Oh well.' A response is expected, so I had better come out with one. 'I suppose there are more incestuous things than marrying somebody whose friend's sister you once had a very brief encounter with.'

'In a town this size, you'd better believe there are more incestuous things.

'There were four or five of them used to knock about together: Angela Crow, Jessica thingumajig, Sharon Rafferty and a couple of others. What were their names? Haven't thought about them in years: where do they all go? Jessica, Pete and I must be about the only ones left.'

'That's not much good. I had Jess down as prime suspect, but now you're telling me there's three others might be just as pissed off about how Isla treated their friend Angela.'

Jacqui glances at me sharply.

'An intruder sounds more likely to me, after all these years. Unless the Crows have some enemy we don't know about.'

I didn't really mean what I said, but such ideas have been running through my mind. It's always something personal and never simply a panicking burglar in murder mysteries, after all.

Were I to seriously go down that path though, Angela herself would need to be a suspect. And Kirsty. Except, I can't have her secretly returning to wreak vengeance *and* lying in a shallow grave.

'If you suspect Angela's friends,' Jacqui points out, 'you'd have to suspect me, as well.'

'Well, I don't. Sometimes you just know people are all right.'

'That's true. I had the same feeling about you this afternoon. There's something definitely all right about you. I think that's why I could tell you all that personal stuff last night. Sounds like Jessica had the same reaction to you.'

A compliment from this woman is a compliment indeed.

'Course, if you did suspect me,' she adds, 'it'd serve me right really, after what I said to you in the street today.'

'Forget it.'

I could forgive Jacqui for worse things than that. I hope, all the same, that, in the unlikely event of the police interviewing her in connection with this business, she doesn't bother to mention the conversation that we had the evening before the murders. I certainly won't be seeking their company now, to draw their attention to the circumstances surrounding Kirsty's disappearance. I would prefer them not to come seeking mine either.

I make a deliberate detour tonight, to avoid passing Callum Brae. From a street one level behind it, I notice a snicket, which I think, from my memory of '86, might lead to the back gates of all the buildings in that part of the High Street, including the guest house. That's as close to it as I want to be.

A World Fit For Heroes To Live In

Throughout a mostly wet weekend, details come to me about the murders, via the local paper and Jacqui, Jess and Pete, who are all part of a non-computerised information network to which I do not have access.

It seems that Isla was pushed or thrown down Callum Brae's staircase and that Sandy was basically just knocked over, which was enough at his age. The possibility of coincidentally tragic accidents has been ruled out on account of some traces of a struggle having been found at the top of the stairs.

Newspapers don't tell us everything, of course, but Pete is friendly with a policeman and keen enough to show off his insider information to me at breakfast. This is how I have learnt that the CID are of the opinion that Isla was killed first and Sandy just got in the way. They aren't sure, though, whether she ran into a burglar or whether the attack was personally motivated and the reason, in itself, for the killer's visit to the guesthouse. Neither am I.

It all depends if Isla upset many people. Apart from her daughters and Jacqui and Jess and me. Were those past acts of violence the only way in which she caused offence?

Pete, luckily, doesn't seem to have mentioned to his police mate that I knew the victims. John Crow is likely to be too distraught to have remembered or passed on anything Isla might have told him about my visit. Unless the local constabulary aren't particularly efficient, one of them is certainly doing enough after hours gossiping about the case, or they don't consider, in a town where most people may have known an established family like the Crows, that they can possibly interview all of their acquaintances. I don't think I left my fingerprints on anything in their upstairs lounge, apart from the photo album. They won't dust that. I hope not, anyway, with both witnesses to which day I was actually there being dead.

Is Kirsty lurking somewhere nearby, I wonder? Doubtful. Coincidence is one thing, but both of us returning at the same time yet being unaware of one another? And why now? Why would either sister or Jess go gunning for Isla all these years later?

I'm glad that there's only Jacqui who knows how very recently I found out about the victim's murky past. Otherwise, a police visit would be a distinct possibility.

No description appears to have surfaced of anyone seen entering or leaving Callum Brae in the late morning or early afternoon, during the hours that John was away. He's a fortunate man, in one way at least: a friend called in to walk to the pub with him and saw Isla alive and well when they set off. The Blacksmith's Arms is sufficiently far away from the boarding house to exclude the possibility of his racing back to do the deed whilst he was supposed to be in the toilet. Plus, his friend and the bar staff all swear that he was never out of their sight for longer than a minute or two. So I can only presume that the police are leaving John to grieve in peace, which is something.

'It's not what you expect in a town like this,' Rex says, when I call on him. 'You don't wanner hear what I'd do with burglars who kill and maim people. Costs nothing to leg it, does it? Okay, so I can still run faster than most, but even the fattest crook could go like the fucking wind if he was desperate enough, instead of just lashing out.'

'So your injury doesn't bother you any more these days?' I've often wondered.

'Only up here,' he smiles wryly, tapping the side of his head. 'Why something like that had to fuck up my career. I'm not poor, but look what I could've earned, playing up to '96, '97. Look what the bastards are on now, even at First Division level. What they call the First Division, nowadays. And the money's not really the point at all. To've played all that time, maybe broken into one of the top teams. And I know I could've gone on into management at some level. I wasn't brilliant at that, but good enough. Might've even made the England squad.'

'There's your ray of sunlight then,' I console him. 'You were saved the embarrassment and disappointment of playing for them.'

He laughs.

'You've got a point there.'

Never satisfied, some people. You'd think a bit of glory and quite a lot of money would do. Although they say that peaking too young is bad for one. If I leave it much longer, that's a problem I'll definitely not have to experience.

Unless it was Kirsty. What if she was meant to be the highlight of my life and it wasn't able to run its proper course? Could it be that easy to – how might Rex put it? – fuck up one's destiny?

My brother may be missing the point. Perhaps his children were supposed to be his greatest achievement, but with being so hung up on the superficial stuff that he's had ever since he outshone the rest of his first junior school team, he's been unable to see that.

'You're getting that glazed look,' he says. 'I see it so often when I get talking about this. In the end, everyone gets sick of it except me.'

'No, it's not that,' I tell him, and explain my misgivings about Kirsty's disappearance and the murders. It's good to talk it through with somebody, especially somebody who has never been involved with the people concerned.

'I realise I can't have it both ways,' I conclude. 'Isla can't have killed her and she killed Isla. And it's crap anyway, because she'd never have harmed old Sandy. And why would she have needed to? He'd probably have kept it quiet if he'd seen her shove her mother down the stairs, after what happened when she was a kid.'

'Beating up her own children…' Rex grimaces.

'Yeah, so without saying this business serves her right – it does; that moment of blind terror as she fell to her death, and the impact, if she lived long enough to register it. It's not as if she never caused pain or fear for anyone else.'

'Karma, you mean?'

'If you like. Sandy too, maybe – he killed a wounded man, after all. But the circumstances give him more of an excuse than she ever had for what she did. Some people might think being an alcoholic is an excuse for violence, but not me.'

'No way. You've got to take responsibility for that sort of thing. I used to drink a bit heavier than usual sometimes when our marriage started going wrong, but I wouldn't've if I'd ended up hitting them when I got pissed.'

'Good to hear it' I say. 'And I'm sorry it didn't work out, by the way.'

He shrugs.

'One of those things.'

'What was the problem?'

Rex reacts to the direct question far less defensively than I anticipate.

'I think we both married the wrong person. Don't wanner go into details, but I hope I've surprised you. Bet you thought I'd say it was all her fault.'

'Something like that.'

I smile and he does too.

'Remember what Marvin the Android said about life?'

I scan my memories of *Hitchhikers Guide to the Galaxy*.

'That the answer to it is forty-two?'

'No, that wasn't him. He said; "life: hate it, ignore it, you can't like it". Not that that's my world view, but I can see what he's saying.'

'It's a bit like that line in *Heaven Knows I'm Miserable Now*,' I contribute. '"I was looking for a job and then I found a job and heaven knows, I'm miserable now". Sums up a lot of what you can end up doing in the workforce.'

'I still can't work out why that woman committed suicide because the Smiths broke up,' says Rex. 'I could never fucking stand them; I'll probably kill myself if they ever get back together.'

*

On Monday, I move into Jacqui's. This is not indicative of developments in our relationship, to which I would be the last to object. It was set in motion the day before, when I joined them for lunch and she asked if I would be attending the funeral with her on Wednesday.

'I'd like to,' I replied. 'It's not impossible that Kirsty might turn up, is it? It's just the finances. They might stretch to Wednesday night, I suppose.'

Straightaway, Jacqui offered; 'Come and stay here if you like. You wouldn't need to go as soon as it was all over then; you could hang on and see more of your brother, see if an arrest gets made.'

'Stay as long as you like,' added Carol generously.

'Tim and I will sort that out, thank you.'

Not that any time limit has been set. Presumably, the responsibility for not outstaying my welcome is mine. I have mixed feelings about the whole thing, anyway. I'll enjoy seeing more of Jacqui and the girls, but the arrangement precludes the possibility of anything happening between us unless she initiates it. You don't try that sort of nonsense on when you're a guest under somebody's roof – it would be an efficient way to end up being slung out on your arse, I should think, if you read the signals wrong.

I don't truly believe that I've had any signals from Jacqui (I'd just like to be able to believe it). She's friendly and candid, but she may not be the slightest bit interested. I'm fairly sure that she has only invited me to stay out of kindness, and maybe for the chance of a little adult company around the house.

*

'We're sorry to see you go,' Pete says, as he serves my final Seaview breakfast. I hope that Jacqui has no intention of providing fried food in the morning; the gilt has worn off that particular piece of gingerbread, after five days of it.

'Just a question of money,' I excuse myself.

'Isn't everything? But it's understandable, aye.'

'That Jacqui's a shrewd one,' jokes Jess, delivering a steaming plate of bacon, sausages, black pudding, egg, tomato and fried bread to the dining room's only other occupant, a traveller type (if that occupational description still exists, aren't travellers reps and gypsies travellers now?). 'Sees the gap in the market and opens a new guesthouse. Not that there really is a gap in the market, the way things are round here.'

'Do you reckon Callum Brae will get going again?' I ask her.

'That's up to John Crow, but I'm sure I wouldnae feel up to it if something like that happened to Pete. And nobody else in the family wanted it; cannae see the likes of his brothers or sisters or Angie coming back to run the place with him. She's too level-headed for that – she's got her own life, and look what going to live in that place did to her mother.'

'They'll never sell it,' predicts Pete, with gloomy relish.

'Don't suppose I'll be seeing you at the funeral?' I ask casually.

'Terrible business, that' murmurs the traveller/rep politely.

'No' me, you won't,' states Jess emphatically.

That, I remind myself, does not make her the killer. I'm having a lot of difficulty seeing her in that role, and I should think that, if it was anybody they knew, that person would attend their funeral, to avoid arousing suspicion.

'I might go,' says Pete. 'I chat to John in the cash and carry and the pub now and again.'

Not that that automatically makes him the murderer, of course, either.

Glamis

It's Tuesday, and Rex has brought me to visit Glamis Castle. The rain is lashing down and we have to run from his car to the entrance. He pays for both of us to get in, which is just as well – it's a hell of a price.

This is one of the more impressive stately homes that I have seen, made of the pinkish stone which has been used for so many of the buildings in this area, and including amongst it's attractions: a stuffed bear, a haunted chapel, a sealed up gaming room and the fact that the Queen Mother grew up here. A woman who lived to be not quite as old as Sandy Crow. It must be something in the water around here, or a mysterious force given off by the pink stone.

After the tour, we linger over coffees in the cafe. We're in no hurry to get soaked again; I pity the poor Highland cattle in the field adjacent to the car park.

'How do you feel about those people who died?' Rex asks, stirring sugar into his second coffee.

'Do you mean the Crows?' I check. A fatal plane crash, somewhere in the world, was reported on last night's news. We never have to wait too long for a fresh dose of tragedy, do we?

'Yeah. I've never known anyone who got killed like that. Be worse if it was someone you knew really well, of course.'

'Well, it would have to be. But since you ask, I feel sorry for the old bloke, having such a long life end that way. By the way, are there an especially high number of people a hundred and over, in this area?'

'I dunno. What about Morag or whatever she's called?'

'Isla. Yes, it bothers me, two days after I was drinking tea and looking at wedding photos with her, walking up and down those same stairs with her. But not as much as it would've done if I hadn't found out what she did to Kirsty.'

'That must've been bloody horrible for you.'

'It is,' I confirm. No past tense about it. Anybody who treats children the way that Isla did is despicable. Jess is right: death doesn't alter a thing.

'You and Kirsty... it was an affair, right?'

'Yeah.'

I'm still not comfortable, touching upon a subject like this with Rex. I never was before. Apart from anything else, he was always so much better than me at attracting women. Of course, he had obvious advantages.

To be honest, one reason that I'm in no hurry for he and Jacqui to meet is that I can't help worrying about the possibility of each of them liking what they see, resulting in wild copulation between them at the first opportunity. I wouldn't need that and nor would the fragile new relationship I'm building with Rex. Just as well this isn't a TV programme: they wouldn't be able to resist turning the situation into a love triangle, with my forlorn attempts to keep those two apart as the comic relief.

'You obviously still like her.' Rex is talking about Kirsty. 'Fancy having to find out that something like that had happened. A girlfriend of mine once told me she'd been sexually abused. That's even worse. I didn't handle it very well.'

'It wouldn't be the easiest thing to handle.'

'No,' he stares into space for a few seconds. 'Looking back though, I can't believe my arrogance. I acted like I was the one who was hard done by over the whole thing.'

He shakes his head. 'Ex-girlfriends, eh? You could really let yourself get guilty if it'd do any good.'

What about ex-wives, I wonder, as we walk back out to the four-wheel drive. The rain is easing.

*

We end up in the Commercial, where Rex gets back onto his hobbyhorse of Grandma Wharton's family. Locally based salmon fishers, apparently.

'Imagine trying to make a living at that nowadays,' he smiles, that enthusiastic gleam in his eye, as it was when we discussed this last week. 'They were at it for a few generations. What must it've been like in those days, trying to make a living, just having to get by on your own resources when that didn't happen?' Then he seems to sense that he has my extremely divided attention, and changes the subject. 'Any ideas on this dream girl of yours, then? What do you really think happened to her?'

I was actually daydreaming about Jacqui, but Kirsty is no further from my thoughts than usual, these days.

'Wish I could answer you that,' I say. 'I can't help the feeling that somebody round here must know. Trouble is, they may not know any more – they might be lying in the morgue.'

'We've been through all this. Don't you think the most likely bet is that she's still alive, in some other town or country, and that she had nothing to do with those deaths?'

'Probably. I just feel as if there's some sort of link between her and that though, that I'm totally missing. Don't ask me what it is. If it's a person, I don't know who. I can't come up with a plausible third party who might've done for the lot of them.'

'Don't tell me you're hoping to "solve the mystery"?'

Rex has always had the ability to suggest inverted commas with a slight inflection of his voice.

'Realistically,' I confess, 'I know it's two mysteries, and whatever the police manage to come up with at Callum Brae, I'm depressingly well aware that I'm not likely to ever know what happened to Kirsty.'

'That'll be famous last words if she shows up tomorrow.'

'Do you think she will?' I ask, realising that it's a relevant question.

'How can I say? It was just an idea.'

He doesn't seem to see the relevance.

'Yes, but what I mean is, would you go down to Mum's funeral, if Joe rung me and said she'd just died?'

'Ah, I see.' He spends a few seconds in contemplation of this scenario. 'Not sure,' is his verdict. 'But I'm not Kirsty, am I?'

'Very helpful. Speaking of Mum, any—'

'Not yet. I'll let you know when you leave. If your friend of a friend, Jacqui, doesn't decide to keep you on. Another beer?'

We get talking about the Old Man and the shoe shop. I try to explain how it felt, being considered good enough to take it on only because Rex wasn't able to do so. It's a risk, in view of how he reacted to my messing it up, but he shrugs it off as water under the bridge and buys a packet of Winfield's from the cigarette machine. It's weird watching him light up; he was fiercely anti-smoking when he was a young footballer. Tobacco was a tool of the devil, along with anything else capable of slowing him down – that Crystal Palace defender's boot, for example.

Now, apparently, he anyhow, has a Winfield or three sometimes when he's out drinking, and throws the rest of the packet away, so that they don't become a habit.

The way the other half live.

In The Midst Of Life

Jacqui is all in black again. A suit this time. I'm finally getting to see her in a skirt, one that finishes just above her knee. She has amazing legs. When some people say that, they mean that a woman, generally blonde, has thighs that seem to go on forever. That isn't what I mean though. Perhaps I can best sum up my feelings like this: watching the muscles at the back of Jacqui's knees in motion, when she walks, is quite an experience.

She has the whole day off work, and we are planning to spend much of it together. I'm tempted to think of this as our first date; she asked me on it after all. It's just a pity that it's actually a double funeral.

We drive to the eleven o'clock service in her mini metro. It isn't being held at Saint Andrew's, the Presbyterian church in the High Street, but at the crematorium on the edge of town.

This doesn't seem fitting for someone of Sandy Crow's age. I find myself thinking about the sergeant he shot, who, along with most of the men who went over the top beside them that day, will probably have a generic headstone in France with: 'A soldier of the Great War. Known unto God' inscribed upon it. Sandy was a lot luckier than those others, but at least they have proper graves.

We get there in good time. From the backmost pew, we watch people filing in. It isn't a bad turn out; there are quite a number of townspeople, whose names Jacqui whispers to me as they pass. It's a bit like when one starts working on a large staff and is taken round and introduced to everybody immediately: pointless, but good manners.

The name Sharon Rafferty rings a bell, as does the petite, bespectacled woman with a short, copper-coloured ponytail, to whom it belongs, but I have to ask Jacqui why this is. 'Friend of Angela's,' she reminds me. (That's right, she was one of her bridesmaids.) 'Still quite close, I think. Lives in Glasgow now – works in the Procurator Fiscal's Office.'

Whatever that is. Still, everyone has a story.

This is certainly true of the Crow family, as they arrive. Sandy's two daughters and two elder sons all appear to be in their sixties and early-mid seventies, and bring an assortment of spouses and offspring with them.

'That's Kirsty's uncle Gordon,' whispers Jacqui. 'He's supposed to have been arrested for brawling in every pub in Dundee except two.

'Gavin, the youngest and best looking of her generally much older, much uglier cousins, wouldn't you agree, so far?'

'Definitely.'

I'm amazed that this bunch have sprung from the same gene pool as Kirsty and Angela. Whatever else she was, Isla certainly injected some badly needed good looks into the family.

Jacqui grins and moves a little closer to my ear.

'That's the reassurance I need. Gavin and I fucked on the beach at Angela's wedding.'

'This is a church,' I say, pretending to be shocked by her language, in order to hide the fact that I am a bit shocked.

'No, it's the crematorium chapel. I widnae swear in the kirk,' she replies, hamming up her Scottishness. 'We just got talking at the reception – he asked if I wanted to share a joint with him. It'd been years; Don and I gave that up before we got married. He'd left me a few months before, the girls were with Mum and Dad for the weekend, and you know how, once you say why not to one type of experience, it can roll over into another type? That's what I've found, anyway. And Don was gone, the girls were away – it was like there were suddenly no rules any more. Nothing to stop me being up for a bit of rec sex.'

'Wreck sex?'

'Recreational. Not something I've got round to again since.'

'Never know your luck,' I tell her. 'You might score at the wake.'

'Tim…' she admonishes me, in the manner of a lady who would not dream of touching on such a subject immediately before a funeral service.

John, Angela and her husband have been sitting up at the front since before we arrived. She has an arm around her father's shoulder, and he suddenly leans his head on hers.

I can almost feel his pain from here.

No Kirsty.

I certainly will not be asking her bereaved family any questions about her. Jacqui has offered to subtly sound Angela out if it seems appropriate. It has to be highly unlikely that she'll know anything.

Who else is missing today? Anybody who looks the right age to have been a lifelong friend of Sandy's. He must have outlived his entire generation. No old soldiers to form a guard of honour.

From the corner of my eye, I see somebody walking in. I whirl around, wondering if this will be like the scene, immediately before the credits roll, where the prodigal makes a dramatic late entrance after everyone has given them up. But no, it's only Pete MacCallum from Seaview, who nods as he slides into the pew beside us.

The service begins. The minister talks for a while about the tragedy that has taken Isla, a devoted wife and mother, and Sandy, one of Craigston's oldest residents, boarding house keeper of long standing, World War One veteran, etc. He may have had a nodding acquaintance with them I suppose, if he has any length of service in the town. It's strange to think that, little as I might have had to do with the family overall, there are things I know about them that their neighbours, and even many of their relatives, don't.

We sing a couple of unfamiliar Presbyterian hymns, pray a bit, then the coffins begin their journey along the conveyor belt. As always, I am unable to relate to the fact that the bodies of human beings whom I knew are inside them.

Other people appear to have no such difficulties. John is openly weeping. Who wouldn't be, watching their loved ones trundling away like that? I doubt that I'd have even been able to make myself turn up, if it was say, Mum and... Rex? Linda a few months ago?

Now I'm depressed. How ideal for a funeral.

John and Angela are both crying as they walk past us on their way out of the crematorium. Angela's blond, handsome husband is dry-eyed but solemn looking, as befits a male in-law on such an occasion.

'Are you going back to Callum Brae?' Pete asks us. 'They're putting on a bit of a do. No guests there now, of course, so I suppose they'll use the dining room. I'm no' sure how we'd go about holding something like that in one the size of ours.'

'Do you want to?'

I'll just go along with whatever Jacqui chooses to do.

'No,' she replies. 'But I should. It's part of paying your respects.

'How's life treating you these days, Pete?'

'Aye, fine. Could do with a bit more business, but who couldn't? Same with that outfit you work for, I suppose. You two wanting a lift at all?'

'No, thanks. We'll see you there.'

'Funny to think of him being at Isla's funeral' Jacqui comments, as we get into her car. 'She'd've ripped his balls off if she'd known he shagged Kirsty underage.'

★

He was right about them using Callum Brae's dining room. They have probably had the caterers in; there's a lot of food to choose from, although no alcohol. Jacqui and I take a polite paper plateful each and stand a little to one side, feeling awkward. At least, I do. Everybody else here is probably a relative or someone who lives in or originates from Craigston. My only two real connections to the Crow family are absent, one vanished, one burning right now. I feel like a gatecrasher.

Jacqui makes conversation with a few people, introducing me as simply a friend of hers from England, as though that would not be assumed anyway, as soon as I open my mouth. Whilst she chats, I surreptitiously watch her, in her funereal finery, and think what a stupid man Don must be. I wonder, as I shake hands with Kirsty's cousin Gavin and his fiancée, whether he regrets his choice at all, at this precise moment.

Angela is doing the rounds and eventually gets to us. John seems to have vanished upstairs or somewhere.

'Thanks for coming, Jacqui,' she says, a little pink around the eyes. Eyes which, although she resembles her mother in build and colouring, have a distinct look of Kirsty coming and going in them, as she speaks.

'I'm really, really sorry,' Jacqui says. 'Tell your dad... I dunno, tell him I'm sorry, I suppose.'

'I will. You'll not see him again today – Uncle Gordon's taken him to the Blacksmith's Arms.' She shakes her head. 'His answer to everything.

'Thanks for coming. It's always good to see you, even under these circumstances. I always think of you as a sort of cousin.'

Has anyone told Gavin that?

'Angie!' Pete from Seaview has been chatting to Sharon Rafferty, on the far side of the room, but now he's striding over to us. 'I've to be getting back, love,' he says. 'Sorry Jess couldnae be here.'

'It's all right, Pete, I understand how she felt. Tell her I'll be in touch next time we're up here. It won't be long.'

The sullen teenager of my dim recollection has certainly blossomed into a decent woman, in spite of all that rough treatment at a formative age.

'Angela,' Jacqui begins, 'it's a stupid question, but, you haven't heard anything about Kirsty, have you?'

Angela's mouth, a similar shape to her sister's, tightens.

'No. It's still like she's gone to another planet or something.' She turns unexpectedly to me. 'Are you the one who's been looking for her?'

'Oh, yeah. Tim Wharton.' We shake hands. My name and face do not appear to have raised a flicker of recognition. There isn't much reason why they should, especially at so stressful a time as this.

'Where do you know her from again?' Angela asks.

'I was up here for a while – long time ago – we made friends. Stayed here, actually.'

'Did we think she went off with you, at first? Was that you?'

'That's me.'

'And have you come up with anything at all?'

'No, but I mean, where do you start, really?'

'Exactly.' Angela's face softens again, although she isn't

actually doing any smiling today. 'If you ever do manage to find her, well, she'll probably tell you not to tell me where she is. But would you give her a message from me?'

'Of course.'

'Tell her… it was often difficult being her sister, and it wasn't as hard on me as the others when she went, and now I often feel like an only child. But what I'd really like is for the two of us to get some sort of adult relationship worked out, if we ever get the chance. Kirsten probably wouldn't believe how much I'd like that.'

She's crying again and whilst Jacqui puts her arms around her and offers words of comfort, I feel a definite empathy towards this younger, less extraordinary sibling, even more so than I did when Jess was talking about her. Her words could almost have been a description of Rex and I. Only, we have been given our opportunity to sort things out. Angela may actually have been an only child for the past seventeen years.

We slip away soon after this.

'She's nice, isn't she, Angela?' I say.

'I didn't used to like her when we were young,' admits Jacqui, 'but I've a lot of time for her now. She doesn't deserve any of the shit she's had in her life. Neil seems to have worked out a decent sort of husband, so far, thank God.'

'It's such a pity Kirsty wasn't there.'

'I keep getting this awful sort of feeling, like it was her funeral we were just at. Don't ask me to explain it.'

And don't ask me to. Jacqui's slightly psychic and Kirsty's very dead?

We pull up outside her house, behind a familiar looking vehicle. Rex is at the door, about to place an envelope in the letterbox.

'That's my brother,' I explain.

'He's gorgeous.'

Thank you, Jacqui.

'Tried ringing, then I remembered where you'd be,' says Rex. 'I was gonner leave you this. I'm shooting over to Edinburgh for a few days, back at the weekend.'

He is openly looking Jacqui up and down, on a public

pavement.

'Got time for a coffee before you set off?' she smiles.

Were she a less sophisticated woman, she'd be giggling and playing with her hair.

'Thanks, Jacqui, but I'd better get going. Maybe we can all get together after I get back.'

'That'd be great,' she says.

'Yeah, great,' I agree.

I'll swear she stands further back than necessary from the door, so that she can bend to unlock it and send Rex on his way with a pleasant image of her tight-skirted bottom fixed on his retina. He toots and she turns, smiles and waves.

How could I have been so right?

I realise for certain as she's making the coffee that it's never going to happen for me with Jacqui. I was stupid to think there was a possibility that it might, without a shred of evidence to support the theory, beyond the fact that she didn't recoil hissing at the very sight of me.

But then, this seems to be what I've become like, since Linda began to withdraw from my life. Wanting to see Kirsty so much that, hey, here I am, transferring onto Jacqui that which I must have transferred onto Kirsty's memory from Linda in the first place.

What good would it have done me if Kirsty had been back around? Why would she necessarily have wanted me suddenly turning up? Would she have even remembered who I was?

'You're quiet,' Jacqui says, as I drink coffee and try not to look at her legs. 'Thinking about the funeral?'

'Partly. I'm still trying to work out how I'm supposed to feel about the death of a child beater and a murderer.'

'Welcome to the club. Hey, hang on, what do you mean "murderer"? Isla never killed anyone.'

'No, not her.'

Not as far as I know.

'You aren't still on this stupid thing about Kirsty being killed, are you?' It's a possibility which I have raised with her again since I came to stay, and Isla's name has been floated, but Jacqui has remained sceptical. 'You haven't any proof and she really wasn't like that any more by then' she reminds me.

'I said, not her. Sandy. He killed his own sergeant in the First World War. Kirsty told me about it.'

This is something which I haven't mentioned to her before. I have always felt as though it was a confidence, and I take those seriously. Even with Sandy dead for five days, Rex is the only person I have ever told, until this moment.

'You sure she didn't say a German sergeant?' Jacqui double-checks. 'Wouldn't it be like an own goal, otherwise? And how's he supposed to have got away with it?'

I tell her everything I know about it.

'Not really murder though,' is her judgement.

'It probably was, but I know what you mean. In a situation where your job involves killing people, the circumstances are a bit more mitigating. When Kirsty told me, she said her grandfather said to her that the thing you learn from killing is that it's easy.'

'Yeek!' Jacqui grimaces. 'Probably true though. And Kirsty's the one he'd've told stuff like that to, if anybody. They used to be so close. He was all she had really, in that house.'

The telephone rings. She picks it up and makes a number of brief replies which give nothing away, then concludes with; 'Yeah, that's fine, we're both here now, come right round. Got my address? Oh, of course, the phone book. Okay.

'That was Sharon Rafferty,' she tells me. Why this seems to have made her excited, I don't know, but that is my immediate impression.

'Angela's friend?'

'That's right. Angela apparently told her we were trying to track Kirsty down. Said she didn't want to bother Angela with it at a time like this, especially if it leads to nothing, so she wants to talk it over with us.'

'Talk what over?'

'Oh, sorry. She thinks she might have some information about Kirsty.'

Sharon

Whilst we're waiting for her to arrive, we try to guess what Sharon might have to tell us.

The popular favourite ends up being that she has run into Kirsty in Glasgow, or thinks that she might have glimpsed her, but wasn't sure whether it was her or not.

The doorbell rings.

Sharon has large hazel eyes and a suggestion of freckles peeking out from beneath her make up. They are clearly visible at her throat and lightly scattered across her legs. Like Rex before with Jacqui, I am meeting her at a time when, thanks to her funeral outfit, she makes the maximum visual impact. She's wearing a silk blouse, miniskirt and small, pointy boots in about a four – all of which are black.

'Sad day,' she comments, to break the ice.

We agree. What else are we likely to do? Apart from screaming: 'Yes, but what have you come to tell us?'

'This might be nothing,' she says, without further preamble, as she takes a seat on the couch. 'See what you think.'

'Have you seen her?' asks Jacqui impatiently.

'Oh no. I'm not sure I'd recognise her by now, if she's changed much. Might do though, she was so pretty.'

She's preaching to the converted on that one.

'My parents are in Greece at the moment,' she informs us, 'so when I got here last night, I stopped at Tesco's to get a bit of food in; I'm here till the weekend – felt like a few days off. Who should I run into in there but Glenda Mitchell.'

'Was she your teacher too?'

'No, but she plays bridge with Mum and we know each other. Stopped for a chat, like we do. Got talking about the murders, naturally. I said I hadn't seen Angie yet, with me living in Glasgow and her Auchtermuchty, but that I thought she'd be taking it hard—'

'Is Auchtermuchty a real place?' I can't resist asking. 'I always thought it was just a made up, typical Scottish sounding name.'

''Course it's real, it's in Fife. Let Sharon tell the story,' Jacqui all but growls.

'Well, Glenda Mitchell said, "what about Kirsten?"' Sharon bestows a significant look upon us both. 'I said, "oh no, she's out of touch with her family." Glenda said – and I'm trying to remember this word for word – "that's understandable after what she went through. She's probably better off where she is now."'

'What was that?' Jacqui demands. 'She said, "where she is now"?'

'Not "wherever she is now"?' I suggest.

'Definitely "where": I only thought about it afterwards. For a start, saying she was better off made it sound like she knew about...'

'The violence,' supplies Jacqui.

'Exactly. I thought you'd know, but I'm sure none of us who were their friends would gossip it about. Could you imagine Kirsten confiding in Glenda? She was your teacher?'

'No way. She hated Mrs Mitchell.'

'So what could she have meant?' Sharon asks, '"better off where she is now."'

'Sounds like she knows where Kirsty is.'

'Oh, that's ridiculous,' cries Jacqui. 'She's not going to be ignoring everybody else, but ringing Mrs Mitchell up for a chat. And I'm bloody sure she was never on her Christmas card list.'

'It did sound like she meant that, Jacqui.'

'I think I'd better go and have a talk with her,' I decide.

'Well, I wouldn't go round to the school and burst into her office,' advises Jacqui. 'God, can you imagine, Sharon, what she'd do to anyone who did that, unless it was a minister or the Queen or something.'

A moment later, they're giggling together like schoolgirls at the mental image of my being torn limb from limb. A necessary release of nervous tension, perhaps, on such an emotional day?

Is it bollocks. It's simply that most people, if you scratch the surface a bit, have never really stopped being kids.

'My God,' laughs Sharon. 'Try to be tactful. Glenda's a tough lady. Nobody took chances around her at school.'

'Except Kirsty,' Jacqui says.

'Oh, that's right. She was always getting into trouble, wasn't she? Angie was actually talking to me about that not so long ago, and she was saying how embarrassing it used to be for her, because kids used to make fun of her for having a sister who misbehaved. She said she had a real go at Kirsten about it once, after she'd heard about her being smacked at school again, but it was a waste of time. Apparently, Kirsten just said, "Who cares? I know how to handle shitty things when they happen to me, even if you don't. And what's the big deal? Anyone can cope with a sore bum."'

'Apart from the type you get by giving birth and having half a dozen stitches,' says Jacqui.

'Ooh, don't.'

Sharon crosses her legs.

'I'll go and visit Mrs Mitchell at home tonight,' I decide. 'Anyone know where she lives?'

'Quite near me,' replies Sharon, 'Rosemount Gardens.'

'Will you be able to direct me there, Jacqui?'

'Yeah, sure.'

'Look, I need to get going,' Sharon announces. 'Why don't I take you there now, so you know it by sight? Long as you don't mind walking back.'

'Good idea, thanks.'

'Sure you won't have a coffee?' Jacqui offers.

'That's all right. I do need to be away. But thanks and it was nice talking to you.'

'You too. How's life at the PF's Office?'

'Fine.'

'And you're not married yet or anything?'

'No,' Sharon smiles. 'Few reasons for that, but I think the best one is, I'm still only thirty-one.'

'Good for you. See you again.'

'See you, Jacqui.'

'Back soon,' I tell her.

★

'Well,' says Sharon. 'How did this happen?'

It's gone eleven p.m. and I still haven't visited Mrs Mitchell. Clearly, I will not now be doing so until tomorrow.

I could answer the rhetorical question. I could tell Sharon how it happened.

She drove me through Rosemount Gardens and pointed out the Mitchell residence. Then she asked if I would like to continue to her parents' house for coffee. With time to kill and a definite liking for her company, I said yes. And of course, I do enjoy coffee.

'This is it,' she said, pulling up in the driveway of a semi with black wrought iron gates. 'As a person with a responsible clerical position in the PF's Office, it would be better if my mum and dad lived in a slum and I was a self made woman, but there you go.'

'My old man was a successful retailer,' I told her, 'you can never rely on them.'

Then there was that moment. We were making eye contact, but for too long, and neither of us seemed to be able to shift the direction of our gaze. And a strange, almost buzzing – or humming – sensation was creeping over me; one which I had not experienced for a very long time.

Sharon reached out, pulled my head towards her, then swiftly turned away and sneezed.

'Shit, sorry,' she gasped, twisting in her seat and digging frantically under her skirt, whilst I hoped that she wasn't allergic to me and took in an exquisite view of her red panties.

'Sorry,' she repeated, after blowing her nose. 'It was starting to run. I hate these sort of outfits; even my shirt hasn't got a pocket. Nowhere to stick your hanky but up your knicker leg.'

'That's okay,' I told her, and by my standards, it was. I spent eleven years with a woman who never learnt how to sit decorously in a short skirt or dress. Linda told me once that it wasn't a priority, as in her line of business, such carelessness equalled free advertising. I think she was joking. I certainly hope that she was; anyone prepared to be caught in those ridiculous cotton things with the dancing teddy bears on them, which she wore so often, would have been putting commercial interests much too far ahead of personal pride.

'Let's go into the house,' Sharon suggested, after we had tried the whole thing again, with greater success. 'I think my parents would rather we did this in their bed, not the drive, if they had to choose.

'It's funny,' she said, unlocking the back door. 'I thought this was probably what I meant by "coffee" but I was still deciding.'

'You were deciding?'

'Oh, well, I knew you were up for it. It's always easy to spot interested parties when I go out wearing my legs. Not that that makes me special; it's the same for plenty of women. Jacqui Bassett for a dead cert.'

Really? If she was able to spot the 'vacancy' sign lighting up in my eyes, it can't have appealed to her. But never mind that.

'She's already had one bloke I know mentally undress her since the funeral,' I said, taking Sharon in my arms.

'Yes, well, that happens, of course. All part of the package.

'Hang on a minute, you're fogging up my glasses.'

We didn't have coffee. Or any food. We didn't seem to need it.

We did not go straight to her parents' bed, either, but we're there now, with it being the only double in the house.

At one point, right in the middle of things, her mobile phone began to bleep. She simply fished in her handbag for it, freed her mouth and said: 'Rafferty.' Something which I would find incredibly pretentious if it came from a person I didn't like, but the names Sharon and Rafferty are music to my ears just now, together or apart.

'I should've really rung Jacqui,' I say. 'Too late now, with children in the house.'

'She won't be bothered, will she? Why should she? I'd be surprised to hear there was anything going on there.'

'Oh no, no chance of that. She's just been a really good friend, putting me up, telling me a bout Kirsty.'

Sharon smiles.

'Well, I won't ask if there was anything going on with you and little Ms Crow. It's no business of mine, and anyway, it's totally obvious.'

★

Late on Thursday morning, we finally drink coffee. In the lounge, with the central heating on, but no clothes. Sharon pads backwards and forwards to the kitchen, her now loose mop of hair swinging behind her, as she repeatedly checks on some sort of brunch she is preparing.

She has freckles everywhere that the sun has been. She isn't a naturist, and 'Exhibit A' in her defence has to be her surprisingly fat, clear-skinned bottom, with its saucy early cellulite dimples, which give it an interesting, lived-in look.

Also pristine white are her small breasts, with their pink nipples, which seem to have discovered the secret of permanent erection.

Her pubic triangle is also Defence 'Exhibit A', this time in the case of her hair being its natural colour. Linda dyed hers all kinds of different shades during our years together, but like me, she was fair really, and both of us have pubes which appear unflatteringly grey in the wrong light.

Sharon's, on the other hand, are bright chestnut, and quite the most beautiful that I have ever seen.

The Educator

'Where were you last night?' Natalie demands, when I arrive back for dinner.

Both girls are looking questioningly at me, with Jacqui standing behind them, smirking and making suggestive pelvic movements.

That's good; she isn't put out in any way by my absence.

'Sorry,' I tell them. 'I got a bit busy.'

'Well, we all need to keep busy,' says Jacqui innocently.

'That's right,' Natalie agrees, truly innocently.

'Hope you don't mind,' I venture, when we're alone in the kitchen. 'It got too late to ring you. I'll be there again tonight, just so you know this time.'

'No, look, you've contributed to the food; it's up to you whether you're here to eat it. And I can't blame you going where you don't have to sleep on a couch, although I'm sure the bed wasn't the main attraction.

'I'm happy for you. Took me a while to work out what was going on, but when I did, I was surprised, but happy. She was always a nice girl.'

'Thanks, Jacqui.'

'I could wring your neck as well though, leaving me guessing about what Mrs Mitchell said.'

'Oh, hell, sorry. The only thing is, I haven't been yet. I'll be going there tonight.'

Jacqui rolls her eyes.

'I get it! Maybe if girls were my thing, I'd even be able to understand it. Should've gone myself. Fair's fair though, I suppose; if I'd been on my way there and Greg Wise had come along and offered to whisk me round to his parents' empty house, I wouldn't've made it either.'

'I'll ring you about it afterwards as soon as I get round to Sharon's. Promise.'

Jacqui does a quick glance around, to ensure that neither of the girls have drifted back within earshot, then says softly:

'You fucking better.'

*

'Good luck,' she wishes me later, as I'm preparing to take my leave. 'Whatever you do, if the front door's open, don't just walk straight in. She probably takes a strap to burglars.'

That reminds me.

'No progress yet on Isla and Sandy?'

'No arrests, no.' She gives me another lascivious grin, 'course, you wouldn't've been reading the papers just lately, would you?'

It's great having Jacqui just as a mate, without the pressure of seriously fancying her any more. I hope that if it's what she wants, she finds a boyfriend soon – Greg Wise or whoever – because she deserves to get what she wants, and because I want to rib her back.

Perhaps I could even handle her going out with Rex. As long as he'd treat her right.

"Bye, Carol, 'bye, Natalie,' I call. 'See you at dinner tomorrow.'

They barely look up from *Eastenders*.

'Bring Sharon along tomorrow night,' Jacqui suggests. 'Just don't maul each other in front of those two.'

'As if we ever would. By the way, is there a Mr Mitchell round at Rosemount Gardens, to make this doubly awkward?'

'There was when we were at school, but last I heard, he'd moved on to a new Mrs Mitchell, the way they do. Course, she could have some new love interest on the premises by now. If an old troll like Sharon Rafferty can get herself fixed up, anybody can.'

I really couldn't see Jacqui and Rex working out. Her sense of humour and over abundance of personality might be a bit much for him. They're starting to be for me.

Rosemount Gardens is a couple of miles away. I pick up a chunky Kitkat en route and try to get used to the idea that I may be about to find out where Kirsty is. I end up convincing myself that this will turn out to be a totally false lead, leaving Jacqui, especially, feeling very let down.

Mrs Mitchell with her feathers ruffled is not likely to be a pleasant experience. She'll probably keep me in to re-wallpaper her spare room and send two hundred lines back with me for Sharon to complete by tomorrow morning, as a punishment for not listening properly to what she was told.

The woman who answers my knock is a surprise. She is friendly and polite, an attractive fifty-something in tiny fur-lined slippers, perhaps only a size three and a half. I had her marked down as ferocious and absolutely ancient by now, either close to retiring age or slightly over it and refusing to leave office.

'Something you'd like to talk to me about?' she says, in a melodic Highlands sounding accent, although I could be wrong on that one, I'm no expert. 'Certainly, if you'd like to come in. And you are?'

'Tim Wharton,' I tell her, as I follow her down the hall into a back kitchen which is far newer than the house itself.

'Tim?'

'Yes.'

'Should I know you?'

'No, I'm not an old pupil.'

'I would hardly have expected you to be, unless you'd been away in England since straight after I taught you. Tea or coffee?'

Why does this keep happening? Do these awful women who assaulted Kirsty as a child, legally or illegally, have to be so bloody nice? She isn't making it easier.

'Look, no thanks, Mrs Mitchell, I'd better—'

'Please call me Glenda.'

Give me a break! Can't she order me to address her as 'Madam', like that anally retentive history teacher at my high school used to insist that kids did when they spoke to her? I could deal with this a lot better if she would at least irritate me.

'Glenda, the thing is, there's someone I want to talk to you about.' Then, realising how grim that might sound, I add; 'Oh, it's not one of your children or anything.'

'Yes, I know,' she smiles. 'I haven't got any children. So who is it?'

'Kirsty Crow. You know her as Kirsten, I think.'

And then she changes.

'I'm Scottish,' she snaps, the warmth in her light blue eyes shutting off. 'I'm well aware that Kirsty is a popular diminutive form of Kirsten. I'm sure that someone who spoke English as a second language could instantly work that out.'

'Sorry, I didn't mean to—'

'Can you take Kirsten a message for me?'

'What?'

She is out there somewhere.

You bet I can take a message, Mrs – no, Glenda – no, probably Mrs Mitchell again now. Write it down, along with her address, and I'll deliver it personally.

'Tell her enough is enough. I know I was wrong, but I was hard on a lot of children, and she's the only one who keeps on coming back at me about it. She put on that ridiculous act in the street, years ago, then the letter and now you. Well, whoever you are, let me tell you—'

'I just told you my name.'

She's flipped. This is no good. She has only imagined that she knows where Kirsty is. Driven mad by guilt, or, more likely, years of teaching.

'Yes, I know your name,' she says icily, 'but I mean, whoever you are in Kirsten's life. Tell her to get up here herself and discuss it openly with me. She can even have an apology if that's what she feels she's owed – so long as I get one, for this occasional harassment.'

'Mrs Mitchell…'

'Yes?'

No 'please call me Glenda' this time.

'I swear to you, I haven't seen Kirsty since 1986. I'm here to see if you know where she is.'

'Oh certainly; I'm going to fall for that.'

'Ring Jacqui Bassett and ask her,' I challenge.

'They were friends. She was with Kirsten that time in the street. Tell her I'm disappointed by this.'

'All right then,' I shout, losing patience. 'Ring Sharon Rafferty. You play bridge with her mother. It's only because of what you said to her in the supermarket the other day, about Kirsty being better off where she is now that I'm even here asking you this.'

'Oh. I see.'

The wind leaves her sails immediately, but I decide to press home the advantage.

'I know Sharon's Angela's friend, before you think of that, but the entire Crow family aren't conspiring against you. Half of them are dead and the rest don't know where Kirsty is. Apparently you do, and they could really do to see her at the moment.'

Mrs Mitchell has a go at smiling and waves in the direction of a pair of polished wooden kitchen stools set against a breakfast bar.

'Sit down. I still don't know where you fit into all of this, but I must apologise for my reaction. You now seem well-informed and genuine, so I won't concern myself with what your relationship with these various people might be.'

Just as well. Sharon hasn't given me permission to announce myself as her new sexual partner to someone who plays bridge with her mother.

'I'll be glad to help Angela Crow,' Mrs Mitchell tells me. 'Less so her father, from what I've heard about the kind of home those girls grew up in.'

'No, it was their mother, not him,' I correct her, 'but he apparently did nothing to stop it. He's suffering now, if that's any consolation.'

'Oh. I seem to be getting a lot of this wrong.'

'How do you know about what happened to Kirsty and Angela? Sharon and Jacqui don't think it was common knowledge.'

'No, it wasn't, so far as I'm aware.' She rises from her stool. 'Let me show you something, Tim. Something I keep to remind myself that, even with what's seen as a successful career, I've still made mistakes – in all probability, a lot more often than I realise.'

'You mentioned a letter? Why did Kirsty write to you?'

'She didn't really. But it is a letter by her, as you'll see in a moment.'

She leaves me deeply mystified, but returns almost immediately, with a high quality looking scrapbook. No scratting around, wondering where she left it, obviously. I'll bet she has an extremely well organised study tucked away in here somewhere.

She places the book in front of me on the breakfast bar, open at a two-page spread which includes: a newspaper clipping about Craigston Primary School, complete with photograph of her and posing pupils, and a copy of a successful report on the place by the local education authority. She is drawing my attention, however, to a smaller piece of newsprint. Each item has a date printed beneath it, in her clear, rounded, feminine hand, but this one simply says: '*Late 1999*'.

I quickly read what is obviously a letter to a newspaper.

Sir

In response to Back to Basics' comments in this column, re the issue of reintroducing corporal punishment in schools, here is a case study (s)he could consider. I was educated in North East Scotland, and strapped several times, particularly by one of my teachers. I did not moderate my behaviour on any such occasion to avoid being punished that way again. It was not effective. I was the product of an abusive violent home and feel sure now that this was the cause of my behavioural problems. None of my teachers seemed to be alerted to this possibility. It was obviously easier to strap and slap me. I would never allow my own children to remain in an education system where the clock had been turned back to what I experienced.

KIRSTEN FEENEY

I look at Mrs Mitchell.

'It s very honest of you to keep something like this,' is the best that I can manage.

'Well, before you ask, I can't think of any other Kirsten it's likely to be. There were surprisingly few of them in her generation, around here, at least.'

'Even less of them in our generation in England, from what I remember.'

'Anyone reading that letter would expect it to be written by a much older woman,' she says, staring at nothing in particular, over my left shoulder. 'The teachers of earlier times had more of an excuse; we knew very well that there were other ways, and that not everybody even supported our right to hit children anymore. A lot of teachers at my school still advocated it though – it was a strict, old-fashioned sort of place, almost up to the time I took over as head. We didn't exactly get parents banging on the door complaining, either, so it was just easier, for maybe the first fifteen years I was teaching, to get a reputation as someone who would reach for the strap at the drop of a hat. No wonder Kirsten reacted so strongly to the idea that I'd banned it.

'I can only presume that she's a friend of yours. What kind of woman is she?'

'That's what I'm trying to find out. That letter from the newspaper is the first word anyone seems to have had from her since she was seventeen. I know as much about her as you do, really.'

'Seventeen? Why…' Mrs Mitchell performs some swift mental arithmetic, 'she must be thirty or more by now. How could anybody make their own child so unhappy that she feels she has to do that?'

'Did you keep the envelope, Glenda?' I ask.

'No, I didn't. But the postmark was Leicester. I imagine this is from a paper local to that area, quite possibly a free paper, these days.'

Leicester. I'll have to prise myself away from Sharon in good time tomorrow morning and get back to those phone books in the library.

'I thought about trying to trace her.' What? Is this woman reading my mind? A rough, tough teacher with that skill is all the kids would've needed. 'I didn't though. What could I have said?'

'Thanks a lot for your help, Glenda.'

'If you find Kirsten,' she says, 'tell her about this conversation, if you wish. I don't suppose she'll be particularly impressed, but I want to go on record as saying that I hope her life's worked out well, away from that awful mother – even if I am speaking ill of the dead. She has children and a new name, so let's hope she has a decent husband. I gather that Jacqueline Bassett married a complete bastard.'

I'm as taken aback as I would be if I'd heard one of my own former teachers using a swear word.

'Jacqui's doing fine without him,' I tell her. 'Two lovely daughters.'

Then I worry that I might have been unintentionally tactless. If Mrs Mitchell did not choose a career over children, but had it dictated by nature, she'll be soul searching over that after I leave, the mood I've put her in.

'Bright girl, that,' is all she says. 'Kirsten too; that's why I had so little patience with her, knowing how capable she was.'

As she walks me up the hallway, I attempt to lighten the mood by asking if the pupils have a nickname for her.

'Mitch the Bitch,' she replies, without any real suggestion that she finds it amusing. 'Overhearing Kirsten Crow calling me that was the first thing I ever put a strap across her hand for.'

Just A Quick Chat

Sharon's doorbell rings. Bad timing, I think, you've just missed her. Never mind, this old friend or whoever can come in and wait; she's only slipped out to the shop. We've already used nearly all of the milk that she bought on Tuesday night.

As soon as I open the door, a denim-clad man walks straight into me and shoves me against the nearest wall.

'Stay away from her' he snarls.

I'm terrified, but I take in a few further details about him. Despite the snarl, he's a fairly good-looking bloke. Brown haired and tall. Well, big all over, actually, which is the main worry, from where I'm standing. His shoes are a good size twelve or thirteen.

'Do you hear what I'm saying?' I nod. He sounds Glaswegian. Glaswegian...

'I fucking mean it – stay the fuck away from her.'

'Got it,' I say.

He suspects flippancy and doesn't like it. His face and grip both tighten. Then he simply says; 'Good,' releases my shirtfront and leaves the house as quickly as he entered it.

I'm shaking. I seriously consider sliding slowly down the wall to a sitting position, the way they do in films. My legs seem prepared to continue supporting me though, so I remain vertical, albeit, propped up by the hall wall.

Glaswegian. The very morning after I've spoken to Glenda Mitchell. This is too great a coincidence.

Stay away from her. Don't try to find Kirsty in Leicester or anywhere else, because she is nowhere to be found.

The Glasgow menace and her old school teacher must have colluded in her murder. Incredible though it sounds, I can come up with no less sinister interpretation of this unexpected move against me. Which must mean that the unspecified threat behind his exhortation to stay away from her is that I could end up the same way.

Perhaps they killed Isla and Sandy too. I have no idea why, but I'll let the police work on that. I turn towards the lounge, where the nearest phone is kept.

'Hey, you!'

My feet almost leave the floor. I spin around to face him in less than a second. I'm not having him behind me.

'Remember: stay the fuck away.'

He vanishes again and I soon hear a car engine starting up. By the time I've gathered my senses enough to push the front door shut, Sharon is turning into the drive.

Thank God she wasn't caught up in all that.

Interlude

1st July 1916

Sandy felt, rather than heard, a movement. He glanced frantically around. He ought to have thought harder before he pulled the trigger. If anybody had seen him, he was done for now.

His momentary panic subsided as he established that everybody anywhere near him, on the dusty ground of No Man's Land, seemed either to be dead or unconscious. Men from the earlier waves. His old mate Sam King, over to one side of him. Lieutenant Carter. Sergeant Hay.

He had put an end to the bastard's pain, anyway. He was able to hear men at more of a distance who would die slowly under the Picardy sun, if the stretcher-bearers didn't manage to come out.

Sandy dropped the pistol beside its previous owner.

Nobody had seen him touch it; he was getting jumpy and imagining things, that was all.

He had better get a move on, or the next wave would be on top of him.

Slowly, he stood up and began to walk. He was unhappy with the idea that he now presented a lone target for any machine gunner who was not more immediately occupied by his surviving comrades, whom Sandy could see well ahead of him, at the German wire. The wire that was all supposed to have been destroyed by the bombardment of the previous seven days.

Getting jumpy. That was a laugh. He was going to stay jumpy, on a day like this. Definitely worse than Loos. Cocked up by the bloody generals again.

The hell with them and their directives, now that he was on his own. He leant into a half crouch and started forward at a zigzagging run. It wasn't easy, with so much equipment, and the emotional exhaustion that he was feeling, but there was no sense in being any more of a sitting duck than he could help.

He did not look back. He had no wish to see Hay again. So he did not become aware that Sam King, his body peppered with shrapnel, had raised his head slightly and was watching him.

1st July 1986

Sandy was awake again. He had taken to his bed at half-past nine, when John and Isla came home, but he had not slept for long. That happened sometimes at eighty-nine-years-old. He couldn't complain; he did not seem to need very much sleep now, and he had all night to get it in.

So this was it. The last significant anniversary of the Somme that he expected to see. The seventy-fifth was not out of the question, but there was no reason to bank on it. Or to particularly hope for it. He had had a decent run, and he was becoming continuously more frustrated by his declining physical abilities. Even five years ago, there had not been a lot he couldn't still manage to do for himself, but he was really slowing down now. No heart problems or high blood pressure yet; on the other hand, he didn't have much energy either.

Sandy had never quite made up his mind about God. He had been raised in the kirk though, and between that and his Marion's strong beliefs, he had to wonder if he would not one day be called to account for Sergeant Hay. Shooting a man for hating him, for having his stripe removed on an imaginary charge of incompetence. Those did not seem like the most compelling of reasons now, but he had been proud to be a lance corporal; he had felt that he had earned that stripe at Loos.

He might well be judged for the Germans he had killed too. Why would any God recognise a ridiculous bloody war like that one as an excuse to take life? The conscientious objectors, who had put their religious or humanitarian convictions ahead of their immediate comfort and social acceptability, had been the bravest ones of all.

He had been lucky though, Sandy knew. If anybody had witnessed what he had done to Hay, he would have ended up in front of a firing squad the same month. Considering the kinds of crimes that men were being executed for then, he had to count his blessings after a long, mainly happy life, a good marriage and all of those healthy children and grandchildren.

The things you do, Sandy mused, when you're expecting to die soon. Shooting people. Telling your granddaughter about it.

Getting away with the Hay business had been a useful warning to him never to tempt fate again. Even after the war, when his arm had still been bad and there were no jobs, and it would have been easy to get himself into trouble, he had known better. 'He's a steady one, that Sandy Crow' they used to say.

Life was strange though. In one set of circumstances, a young man could take revenge on an enemy without having to answer for it, but then when he was old and his own kin were the problem, he found himself powerless. He had no longer been strong enough to intervene physically against Isla, when she was knocking the girls about, and he hadn't quite been prepared to go to the authorities and risk seeing the family broken up. He had tried hard to push John into taking some type of action, but he had proved totally useless. It was as if standing up to Isla over leaving the rigs and coming to work at Callum Brae had been the full extent of his capabilities.

Even now that things had improved, Sandy still partially despised his weak, once favourite child and his daughter-in-law. And himself, for giving up, when Kirsty and Angela had had nobody else.

He smiled as he recalled what Kirsty had said to him earlier. His response had been to tell her that he loved her, as well. Their time together was precious – at his age, it had to be fairly limited – and such exchanges were important, even if they did take place so seldom.

Something had happened to her in Glasgow. On what kind of a scale though? Had it been drastic enough for her to learn from, in the same way that he had done after committing his rash act in 1916? Had she even got away with it, as he had?

Sandy didn't know and he was not going to ask. He would have liked her to confide in him, as she had sometimes done as a child. Something was definitely worrying her.

★

Not a lot was worrying Kirsten at that moment, two floors lower. She was listening to *Walking on Sunshine* on a small radio/cassette and quietly coming.

She had experienced this sensation any number of times in Callum Brae, but never before with somebody else in the room.

Afterwards, she clamped her upper thighs tightly around Tim's hand. Her red poppy tattoo completely disappeared from view.

'Do you want me to stop now?'

'No way!' Kirsten said emphatically, kicking free the pair of black string bikini briefs which, for some time, had been hanging from one of her feet, like a nylon anklet. 'It's almost fucking unbearable right now, but give me a few minutes and I'll be putting on an internal firework display again.'

'I'll look forward to that,' Tim said.

'There's not a lot of reason why you should, but I will.'

'There's every reason why I should. I'm enjoying myself enough even without that, just looking at the wonderful Scottish scenery.'

'Oh, tut, tut. Comparing an innocent young girl's fanny to our Highlands, islands, lochs and mountains. Not what I'd've expected from you; objectification of the lowest kind.'

'I was talking about your whole body, actually,' claimed Tim truthfully, nonetheless feeling slightly embarrassed at the possibility that the humorously slanted comment could be misinterpreted to that extent.

Kirsten smiled.

'I don't believe you for a minute, but thanks anyway, for your objectification. I'm flattered – even if it is what you say to all the girls. Although I don't think most Scottish landscapes have as much tangled undergrowth as I have. That's the thing up here; it's too cold for us to need to shave our bikini lines. They say you can always pick out the Scotswomen on the beach in Spain or Greece.'

'That's what I like about you,' Tim told her, only half-jokingly. 'Witty as well as intelligent and beautiful.'

Not beautiful, thought Kirsten. *Pretty enough, for all the use that's been*. Witty, sure, she had been working at that for years; humour was still the best overall form of defence that she knew of. Intelligent, yes. And stupid. And self-destructive. And an expert at fucking up everything in which she involved herself, particularly her own life.

Her mind went back to an hour earlier, when she had shown Tim her tattoo. Was it a poppy, she wondered, or the fleur-de-lys?

Then the climb to orgasm began and she put aside such thoughts.

Part Three
What Became Of Kirsty

Revelations

Jacqui makes the telephone call straight after dinner. She wants to be the one to do it. Sharon, Carol, Natalie and I sit watching her, excitedly. And apprehensively, in my case.

To my surprise, this morning, Sharon talked me out of informing the police about the unwanted caller at her parents' house. She said mysteriously that she might be able to find out what was going on, for herself, before I took it any further. I can only presume that she meant via her colleagues at the Procurator whatever's Office. She made me a cup of coffee and disappeared into a bedroom with her phone. I heard her saying something indistinct, then she returned to tell me that she had set the wheels in motion.

I have a nasty suspicion that she's getting off on the drama of the situation.

She suggested that we still look Kirsty up in the Leicester phone book, pointing out that Glenda Mitchell would hardly have gone to the trouble of faking that newspaper clipping, especially as she had no idea that a visit from anybody like me was imminent. In Sharon's opinion, the chances of locating Kirsty, alive and well, were good, and certainly, we found a number listed for M.J. and K.I. Feeney, which Jacqui has just dialled.

'Hello,' she says. 'Does Kirsty live there, please? She does? Great! I mean, would it be possible to speak to her, please?'

We all look at one another.

'She must be there,' Natalie squeaks. Even she realises that this is something big.

'He's gone to get her,' announces Jacqui, an anticipatory gleam in her eye. 'Really polite. Sexy voice.'

Sharon's mobile phone goes off, in her handbag.

'Shit!' she cries. Then; 'Sorry,' to Carol and Natalie, who are grinning at her. She pulls it out and hurries from the room, stabbing at the Talk button and saying; 'Rafferty', as she whisks it to her ear and mouth. 'About time you rang back,' are the last words I hear from her, as the door closes.

'Rafferty,' Carol mimics, holding an imaginary phone.

'Shit! My mobile phone. Rafferty,' improvises Natalie.

'Natalie...' her sister warns her.

'Ssh!' I say, because Jacqui, looking daggers at both of them, is beginning to speak.

'Kirsty? It is you, isn't it? Jacqui Bassett...'

'Yeah, you too. What happened, Mrs Mitchell made a comment to somebody, so we asked her if she knew where you were.

'Yeah. You...? It's so good to hear your voice again. But, look, Kirsty—

'That's okay, I always knew you'd have a good reason. But there's something you need to know. Your mum and your grandad are dead.

'No, what I mean is, they've both been murdered.

'Sorry to have to tell you like this, but... they think it was a burglar... no; it's got a lot worse up here since then.

'Well, you'd've expected him to die years ago, wouldn't you? No, he hadn't really been down off the top floor for years, I don't think. Don't know when I last saw him. Ran into your mum a few months ago.

'It was held the other day. We didn't know about Mrs Mitchell in time to let you know, but—

'Yeah, do you want my number...? You will?'

Jacqui rattles off her address and telephone number.

Sharon returns to the room as good byes are being said.

'She's coming up tomorrow,' Jacqui shouts, one second after hanging up. 'We'll see her in less than a day. Says her husband will be able to look after the kids for the weekend. She's got a good one there.'

'Did she say what time she'd be here?' I ask.

'Well, how could she? Who knows what the traffic'll be like? She talked about leaving first thing, so you could come round in the early afternoon. I'll ring you if she flukes it any sooner.'

'As long as you want me here at the start. You're the one she's expecting to see. She might hardly remember me.'

'Don't be ridiculous, Tim. All this is happening because of you. And Sharon, of course.'

'Oh, I didn't do much,' she asserts modestly. 'And I'll stay out of it tomorrow. Get myself organised for going home Sunday night.'

I'm trying not to think about that. Kirsty is about to come full circle and be superseded by a niftier model for the new century, complete with mobile phone and freckles. Same principle though: the cute Scot who was only able to spend a few days with me.

'Mum,' Carol says, looking aggrieved, 'you didn't even tell her you'd had us.'

'Oh, I didn't either,' laughs Jacqui. 'Never mind, sweetheart, plenty of time for that tomorrow. And you'll both be able to meet her.'

'But you called yourself Bassett. She'll think you're an old maid.'

'There are worse things to be.'

'That's right,' agrees Sharon. 'Take it straight from the horse's mouth, girls – old maids are having a lot of fun these days.

Her telephone – cradled in the lap of her jeans, as if she expected this to happen – rings again.

'Here we go,' she says, and picks it up. 'Rafferty.'

*

'Looking forward to seeing your ex-squeeze?' Sharon asks me that night, as I'm massaging her deliciously freckle-spattered shoulders and back, and the lovely white snowdrifts of her buttocks. She has goose pimples almost everywhere, but it isn't cold in here, with the central heating on.

I was thinking about precisely what she just suggested: what it is going to mean to me to meet Kirsty again, especially now that there's Sharon.

'Well, yes, just to see how things turned out for her,' I say, trying to be as honest as I can. 'You know, see what she's like now.'

'Yes, I'll be interested to hear how you find her. And how Jacqui finds her, after knowing her so much longer. Then there's

Angie.

'Funnily enough, I just spoke to my old squeeze – that call, while Jacqui was talking to Kirsten.'

Do they say 'squeeze' as well as 'guy' in Glasgow, or is that a personal foible of Sharon's? Very mid-Atlantic.

'Really?' I say casually.

At last, some information about that side of her life. I've been wondering how someone like her happens to be unattached, living in a city of that size. Only recently unattached, perhaps.

'Yes. I'd rung him earlier and left a message to call me. That was this morning, actually, while you were drinking your coffee. And when I insisted on the truth, he admitted that he was the arsehole who watched me go out, then burst in and threatened you.'

'What?'

Stay away from her. He was talking about Sharon?

'I'm so sorry, Tim. I called him last night, while you were out, and told him it was over. It had almost come to a natural end, anyway; we hadn't even spent an evening together for about two weeks. I was honestly planning to end it soon, but it turns out he didn't see it that way. I never thought he'd do anything this bloody stupid though.'

'So that was your ex-boyfriend, telling me to stay away from you?' I can hardly believe this. 'Did you have to be so secretive about it? I've been thinking I'd just had my bloody life threatened.'

'Yes, I really am sorry, but I wanted to be sure of my facts before I started casting aspersions, or telling you there was nothing to worry about, when there still could've been. I thought it sounded like that stupid wanker though: the description, the way he was carrying on. Bet you wouldn't've been so overawed by him if you'd known he was only a lawyer.'

'He's a lawyer?'

Behaving like that?

'Unbelievable, isn't it? Works with me at the PF's Office. He's been acting for weeks like he can barely be bothered with me, then this, because I'm the one who finished it.

'Anyway, he's agreed now that it wouldn't be a great idea if he gave us any reason to complain to the police about his threatening behaviour. He's shit-scared of that.'

'Good.'

I'd like him to know what shit-scared feels like.

'In other words,' says Sharon, 'he won't be giving us any trouble in Glasgow, so don't see that as a reason to avoid the place.'

What does she mean by that, exactly?

'No, I won't. But to be honest, once I go back to England, I won't be able to afford regular visits. Maybe you could—'

'Listen, you—' She turns her head, to remind me that she isn't only attractive from the neck down. 'You are interested in finding out what sort of a future we've got, aren't you? You will come back to Glasgow with me, won't you?'

'Yeah, sure, but I'll have to get home and sign on pretty soon-'

'No,' snaps Sharon. 'I've tried long distance stuff and it's crap. One of you always ends up getting with someone else. Well, actually, it was me, both times. So be warned and let's just take a chance. We don't have to live together straight away if we decide not to rush that, once you find a place of your own. But it's got to be Glasgow, because I've got a life there and you're flexible.'

'Wow!' I say. 'This is all a bit sudden.'

'Life can be sudden. I want us to give this a serious try, and I promise you, I'm never, ever unfaithful in committed relationships, on my own doorstep.

'Better tell me right now if you're not looking for any of this.'

'Actually, I am,' I reply. 'And a bit more. What are you like at picking pimples?'

'Another smartarse,' she says, sounding relieved. 'All I ever seem to get.'

Sharon Rafferty. And me. In Glasgow. I've never been there, but they say it's cosmopolitan nowadays, no longer the scary city of the old legends.

Sharon and me. Sharon and Kirsty in one lifetime. This time though, I'm being invited to stay with her. Glasgow on a one way ticket. Apart from the necessity to zip home, give notice on my flat and to Mandy and Bob, transfer my benefit…

And tell my mum. She'll be wondering why I haven't been in

touch by now. She's going to love this development. Never mind, I'll ring her on Monday, when it's a fait accompli.

Rex is going to have to make his mind up this weekend.

Sharon wriggles over onto her back and pulls me down onto her equally interesting front. There are worse places to be.

'I've got such a strong feeling this is going to work out,' she enthuses. 'And all because we're crazy enough to take a chance on each other.'

I don't know about you, I think, but I'd be certifiably crazy if I didn't.

I Can Still get Angry, Even Now I Know She's Dead

I can't believe it's her. This prettily plump woman, with slight crow's feet and short hair dyed blonde. She doesn't make a bad blonde, with those big brown eyes – I've never gone much on the blue-eyed ones – but it's hard to reconcile this thirty-four-year-old with the teenage waif whom I remember so very well. It's as though a new actress has taken over the role.

I only have one photograph of Kirsty, in which she is wearing jeans and a black T-shirt. For a long time now, that is how I have pictured her: black T-shirt, jeans, permanently seventeen. Today it changes. She is clad in a white linen jacket, multi-coloured, knee-length dress and stylish brown sandals, in the expected size five.

She's very late. I've been here for four hours. I've had my tea with Jacqui and the girls, and both of them have gone back out to play with friends nearby, whilst the daylight lasts. Waiting around indefinitely for an adult whom they have never met before, is not their idea of fun.

'Sorry,' Kirsty says. 'Would you believe I left home nearly twelve hours ago? Fucking Firth of Forth Bridge. And all the other usual motorway delays.

'Shit, girl, you're a sight for sore eyes at the end of a long journey.'

She hugs Jacqui and kisses her cheek, the half smoked cigarette held safely out of harm's way, at a jaunty angle. That, at least, is a familiar landmark which has remained.

'Do you mind if I chuck it down on your front path, or shall I take it back out to the street?'

'No, put it down there for now,' invites Jacqui. 'It'll soon sweep up in the morning.'

She brings Kirsty into the lounge, where I have been sitting, watching the doorstep reunion. Our eyes meet for the first time in seventeen years.

'I know you.'

Well, that's a start. It was the possibility of hearing words like that which brought me up here ten days ago.

'Tim,' I remind her.

'Yes, I know,' she says in bewilderment. 'But what are you doing here?'

'It's because of Tim that we found you.'

Jacqui goes on to explain.

'So let me get it straight,' says Kirsty, seating herself opposite me, on the couch. 'You came up here last week to track me down. Why?'

I feel awkward about it now, having to answer this question to her face. Far more so than when I discussed the matter with Jacqui and Rex, or when I tried to explain it to Sharon: she seemed to understand perfectly, in any case.

'I sort of wondered how your life had worked out.'

'Oh. Fine, now, thanks very much. Wonderful husband, son and daughter.' She produces a photo from her handbag. 'Nice house. Decent sort of life all round.

'What about you, Jacqui? These are your daughters on the wall, I take it?'

'Yes,' she laughs, a little nervously. 'Don's too, actually.'

'You got married?'

'And nearly divorced. Won't be long now.'

'Oh,' Kirsty smiles from one to the other of us. 'Lots of catching up to do.'

'Would you like a wine or something?'

'Right now, I'm absolutely dying for a cup of tea.'

'Okay. The toilet's upstairs, if you need it.'

'You know me, Jacqui. Just go wherever I am, whenever I feel like it. And you don't even have to squat behind bushes on the motorway, so I'm fine – went not long ago.

'There is one thing though. I'm a bit too buggered, now I've finally got here, to face seeing my father tonight, after all this time, in these circumstances. Is there any chance of staying here, please?'

'Of course,' Jacqui says. 'As long as that couch is all right for you. And actually, it'll have to be, because I just realised this morning, after you were already on the road, that I forget to tell you that your dad's staying in Auchtermuchty with Angela right now. Sorry, you could've gone straight there.'

'What's Angela doing in Auchtermuchty?'

'She's married to a schoolteacher called Neil. She's a teacher too, actually. That's how they met – both got jobs there.'

'God, so much has happened,' sighs Kirsty. 'I can't believe my grandad lived so long. One reason I didn't get back in touch for his sake, was that I was so sure he'd be dead by the time I got round to it.'

'You never expect people to live much past ninety, do you?' I say.

'No. Hey, Jacqui.'

'Yes?'

An attempt to get closer to the kitchen and kettle – by no means her first – is delayed by the shout.

'There is a reason I didn't get in touch with anyone, even you. I wanted to put everything before a certain point in my life behind me, start again. I've realised since that nothing's as simple as that, but it took me a long time.

'I always wondered if someone would come looking for me one day.' She smiles half-heartedly in my direction. 'Never once imagined it being you.'

'Just give me a minute to make these drinks,' requests Jacqui, 'before you do die for that cup of tea. Then you can tell us. If you want to, I mean.'

'I will, but it's just between us three. No telling my father or Angela.'

'Course not. Coffee, Tim?'

Jacqui successfully vacates the room. It is she to whom Kirsty has mainly been addressing her comments. Let's be honest, she's the one whom Kirsty is truly interested in seeing again. Even after so long, they have an intimacy which partially excludes me. I would have been hard put to imagine it once, but I may just have to struggle to make conversation with this woman on my own.

'Your sister seems very nice,' I try. 'Changed a lot from when I met her as a kid.'

'As I'm seeing her tomorrow, that's good news.'

'She'll be pleased to see you,' I predict, remembering something of the message which Angela asked me to pass on. 'Said she wished you were here at a time like this and that she'd like to have an adult relationship with you.'

'Did she now?'

'Something like that's just happened to me recently, with my brother. We'd been out of touch for years, but we're getting on quite well now.'

'You've got a brother, have you?' enquires Kirsty politely.

She's forgotten. I'll swear that I discussed the Rex problem with her. I wonder how many of the details about our brief time together have eluded her?

'It really amazes me that you came looking for me after all these years,' she announces suddenly. 'I mean, I know I recognised you as soon as I walked in, but to tell you the truth, I don't think I've thought about you for quite a few years.'

I never really stopped thinking about you.

'Well, I'm glad I came up here to try and see you,' I say. 'It's led to so many other things. I've made friends with Jacqui and her girls, tracked my brother and you down and even managed to get a new girlfriend out of it.'

'Round here?' asks Kirsty, in surprise.

Fair enough, I wouldn't have expected lightning to strike twice in the same part of Angus County myself.

'You know her, actually. Old friend of your sister's who Jacqui mentioned before. Sharon Rafferty.'

'Really? She always seemed such a sweet, innocent little kid. And just think, if Mitch the Bitch hadn't made that careless comment to her, I wouldn't be up here now. Congratulations, you've obviously got a perceptive, intelligent lady there.'

I think about passing on what Glenda Mitchell asked me to tell her, but decide against it. Why bore Kirsty with that; she wouldn't want to hear it and why should she?

Jacqui arrives with the hot drinks and biscuits.

'You are saving my life,' Kirsty tells her indistinctly, through a mouthful of Penguin bar.

'Oh, sorry, Kirsty – all those hours stuck in your car. Let me get you a decent meal. What would you like?'

'No, it's okay, I'll get some fish and chips soon. What was that greasy old dump down by the sea front called? Is it still open?'

'No. Wasn't it the Swordfish or something, when you were here? And no, I'll cook something.'

They debate this for a while and the girls arrive home in the middle of it. Kirsty shakes them both by the hand and a deal is eventually struck that we will get fish and chips for everybody before Carol and Natalie go to bed.

'Hey, see what your clever mum did,' says Kirsty, standing up. She perches her right foot on a chair arm and, with a skill obviously born of long practice, raises her dress just high enough to show her poppy tattoo, but nothing more.

'I want one,' Carol demands, turning to Jacqui.

'You'll be lucky, young lady. Ask Kirsty how often she's wished she didn't have that.'

'Here, hang on, Jacqui. What's this assumption that I get into situations where people see it? I'm a respectable married woman.'

Carol grins delightedly and Natalie doesn't, as the humour has gone over her head.

'It was useful when I was giving birth,' Kirsty admits. 'Everyone kept staring at it, which just made me wonder what they usually stare at, if there's nothing else to catch their eye.'

'They don't,' laughs Jacqui. 'It's just another face in the crowd to them.'

'I like her, Mum,' says Carol. 'She's rude and she makes you rude too.'

'I could always do that,' Kirsty assures her.

'Bet you were the rudest girl in your school.'

'Carol,' remonstrates Jacqui.

Kirsty appears to give the matter serious consideration.

'Not the very rudest, I shouldn't think. Definitely the naughtiest though.'

★

The girls are in bed, we've eaten the fish and chips and have started on wine: Jacqui's and a couple of bottles purchased by Kirsty, who has announced her intention of getting pissed tonight and does not want to punch too big a hole in her hostess's stock on hand.

'And now you'll be wanting to know what happened to me.'

It is twilight outside, that late Scottish May twilight, and we haven't put any lights on yet. The setting seems right for a story which already involves violence against children and is to be told by someone who has had two members of her family murdered. Very modern Gothic.

'You know that morning you caught the bus home?' she asks me.

'Yes.'

'I went straight back to Callum Brae afterwards, grabbed my stuff and left. I'd already packed. I was going to have a quick chat with my grandad first, but he must've gone for one of his occasional walks, which was a relief really, 'cause I wasn't even gonner tell him I was going. Obviously, I've wished since I'd seen him that one time more, but at the time it just made it easier to get away, with him gone and my parents busy in the rooms.

'I hitched back to Glasgow. I was due to appear in court there the next day, July the third. I couldn't come back here anyway, for a year after that, because they sent me down.'

Silence. I don't know what to say and neither does Jacqui.

This possibility never occurred to me. She didn't give me any reason to suspect it. She seemed happy over those three days. Her last days of freedom.

And this doesn't account for the other sixteen years of her disappearance.

'You are allowed to ask what it was for,' Kirsty tells us. 'I'd got this job on the bar in a nightclub, when I was there before. They knew I wasn't even old enough to go in there as a customer, but the woman who ran it didn't care, it kept my wages down. Got me out of the squat I was in and into a flat with two others. Shit money though, once you got used to the fact that you were earning at last, so I started taking a bit here and a bit there out of the till. They were always on at us about it being out, anyway. I was stupid though, 'cause my boss set a trap and caught me red-handed. Dragged me through to her office so she could ring the police. I panicked and thought that if I could just get away, leave town, they'd have better things to do than search the country for me, so I punched her in the face and ducked past her. But the assistant manager was coming to see what all the fuss was about, and he grabbed me and kept hold of me 'til the cops arrived, with her dabbing her bleeding nose and swearing blue murder at me.

'So I'm interviewed down at Maryhill and spend two nights and all Sunday in these disgusting bloody cells, with it happening at a weekend. Then I go up on the Monday and get a trial date of July the third and released on bail. I've only been back in the flat a few hours when the bitch from the nightclub rings up, raving about how I've ruined her looks (like she ever had any) and how she's gonner ruin mine. Before I get mine in court, she says, I'll be getting it somewhere else, where there's no witnesses.

'Well, I was shitting myself. Nobody could take an average sort of hiding better than me, but I was imagining my face being scarred, broken bones – something a lot more vindictive than I ever got at Callum Brae. So that was where I hitched back to the very next morning. I broke the conditions of my bail by not telling the police, but I didn't want my parents finding out what I'd done. I thought that if I still turned up in court on the day, they might go easy on me over the extra charge for skipping bail. I'd been warned that I'd probably go inside, even as a first offender, for assault as well as theft in a position of trust, so I decided to face up to what I couldn't avoid, when it happened, and make sure that woman couldn't get her hands on me.

'So I turned myself in at the court, got put in the cells, then the trial was put back because of the new charge. But I still started my sentence that day, on remand, and I was soon back in court being given eighteen months. I pity any poor tosser who goes through that without already having some of the time under their belt. And at least it was only twelve months, in reality.

'So there you are: the shadows of the prison house closed around the growing girl.'

'I had no idea,' Jacqui says. She's looking stunned.

'And it was because I didn't ever want anyone to have any idea, that I stayed away after. It was the worst fucking year of my life; I wasn't mistreated or anything, but it was a boring, miserable place and I often cried myself to sleep and hated waking up from dreams where I wasn't in there. I fully understand why prisoners with long sentences sometimes top themselves, if they can.

'When it was over, I decided to put that and everything before it behind me, and start all over again. For all I knew, my family could've seen a paper with my name in it or reported me missing and had the police find out I was inside, and I'd've just got hell if I came back. So after a couple of days in a hostel, I was off hitching rides down the MI. Seemed like a good time to start somewhere new. My Glasgow friends who'd visited me at first hadn't been near me in months. Nobody inside was going to miss me much if they never heard from me again. There was a girl there I was in love with, towards the end, but she went out of her way to let me know she was only bothering with me because she couldn't get hold of a man, so I didn't think I'd wait around for her to get out and end up with a broken heart, to match the broken kneecaps I'd have by then if my old boss caught up with me.'

'And it worked out, obviously,' I say, 'making that move.'.

She deserved that, for being brave enough to go where nobody knew her.

'Yeah, almost from the word go. The lorry driver who picked me up was going to Leicester, so I thought, that'll do. Decided my whole future, just like that. It was hard at the very beginning though: not knowing anyone, talking so different, grotty hostel, how the cow at the dole office looked at me, because I'd just got out. It wasn't as hard as going inside though, and I soon made friends and got a job in a pub. I just told them I'd worked in my parents pub up here, the Callum Brae; wouldn't've been much point in them writing to my own family for a reference, would there?

'Met Mike a few years later, in the last year of his masters. He encouraged me to go to university, so I've got a BA now. And more importantly, two lovely kids, David and Melissa. And there you are.'

'Does Mike know about your record?'

'Of course. I could never have been in a serious relationship and not told the other person. Him, my two best friends down there, you two and the children when they're old enough – nobody else. I think Mike's family would be understanding about someone being young and silly though, which is more than mine ever would've. All the same, I have been thinking about getting back in touch the last few years, putting it off, letting it slide. Even been up here a couple of times, but we avoided this part of the country. And now it's too late and my grandad spent seventeen years wondering what had happened to me. I honestly thought, when I finished my sentence, that there was such a good chance he'd be dead, that I'd be breaking my silence for nothing if I went back to see my family on his account.

'Stupid, isn't it? The only person I contacted up here, in all that time, was Mitch the Bitch. Couldn't resist it when I saw my letter in print. I expected to get away with sending her something, but that's me – I fuck up a lot.'

'We all do.' Jacqui strides across and sits beside Kirsty on the couch, putting an arm around her. 'Look at me, stealing your boyfriend, messing up our friendship—'

'You didn't steal him; I practically gift wrapped him for you.'

'Well, it did harm at the time, and I was naive enough to think he wouldn't do the same to me one day. Look at you, you've obviously got a brilliant husband. Bet you've told him everything you ever did and he loves you too much to care.'

Kirsty cannot keep the smile from returning to her face as she thinks this over.

'Yeah, there is that. He knows I spent half my teens making out with men and boys and the odd girl, as well as getting bounced off the bedroom walls by my piss-artist mother and wearing knickers with arrows on for a year. All my secrets. He's a great guy, you've got that right.'

'Bet you've even told him about your tattoo, haven't you?'

'Not yet, Jacqui, but I'm going to. I'm thinking of going all the way with him soon, so he'll find out then.'

These two must have been quite a double act in their day, if this relapse into it is anything to go by.

The doorbell sounds. It's Sharon.

'Sorry to barge in, but I didn't want to ring this late because of the kids. I just wanted to catch up with Tim, so when I saw the light on…'

'Come in and have a drink,' Jacqui invites her.

'I don't want to intrude.'

'Away in Rafferty' shouts Kirsty, sounding for all the world as if she's used to ringing Sharon on her mobile. 'It's not like you're a stranger – although you had acne and plaits last time I saw you.'

'Plaits!' I exclaim.

'We've all had them,' says Sharon, with mock hauteur, as she shakes Kirsty's hand. 'You've really changed,' she tells her.

'You too. You've turned into a real babe.'

'Thanks. You're looking great, but so different. I'd've passed you in the street without a second glance.'

'Oh, don't worry,' Kirsty says. 'People who know me well do that too, if they can avoid catching my eye.'

The doorbell rings again.

'Busy night.'

'There was another car came into the street behind me,' says Sharon. 'Looked like it was looking for a park.'

'I'm certainly not expecting anyone else.'

Jacqui opens the door.

'Hello,' he says. 'Sorry to disturb you.'

He is being far more polite than he was the last time I saw him framed by a doorway. My legs begin to tremble.

'Would it be possible to speak to Sharon, please?'

His eyes scan the room behind Jacqui, giving me a swift, hard look, before alighting upon their objective.

Stop it, I will my legs; he's only a lawyer.

'Come in, if you like.' But Jacqui sounds uncertain, as she steps aside for him. She is obviously picking up some kind of atmosphere, emanating from behind her, although not enough to cause alarm.

'No!' Sharon roars, leaping across the lounge. 'You're not coming in.'

'The lady just said I could,' he points out smugly.

'Are you following me?' demands Sharon. 'Have you been sitting outside my parents' house again? Was that where you were when you rung me half an hour ago?'

'You're worth going to a bit of trouble for, Shaz.'

She kicks him hard between the legs. There's a disbelieving silence, even from him, as he sinks to his knees. I feel a secret triumph: I manage to stay upright when I was the one being manhandled.

'Now piss off, Greg, please,' says Sharon reasonably.

Kirsty turns to me, with an air of detached amusement.

'You've got a good one there.'

'Shaz,' Greg says imploringly, as he climbs back to his feet.

'If you don't leave now, I'm calling the police,' she warns him, whipping her secret weapon out of her handbag and poising a threatening finger above its buttons. 'And if I see you in this town again, I'm telling Charlie about all this on Monday.'

'Then you'll never work in this town again,' Kirsty cannot resist.

'As a member of the Procurator Fiscal's staff, who's behaving like a total wanker, he'll never work in any town again.'

At these words, Greg goes even whiter than he has already gone.

'Come on,' says Jacqui decisively, grabbing his elbow and turning him around, 'get the fuck out of my house – it's a miracle if you haven't woken my kids, and you're letting a draught in. And don't bother coming back to thank me for saving your career. I know I'd never risk mine over somebody who didn't even want me.'

He doesn't offer any resistance as she shoves him out and slams the door. We hear his retreating footsteps, then a car starting up, manoeuvring around and coming back past us. Then we hear something else.

'Mum, what's happening?'

Natalie is standing at the top of the stairs, concern etched deep in her pretty features.

'Oh, I'm so sorry,' says Sharon.

'Couldn't be helped, I suppose,' shrugs Jacqui. 'It's all right, sweetheart, there's nothing to worry about.'

'Well done, girls,' says Kirsty, as Jacqui skips upstairs, kisses her worried daughter and carries her back to bed. 'I've lost my tough Caledonian touch, but it's good to see it's still thriving in its native land.'

I wish I had known, when I met him yesterday, that Greg wasn't some Glaswegian mobster, mixed up in murder, who would stop at nothing. His true identity: a lawyer, who would stop at almost anything, and who was already sticking his neck, with its overly large Adam's apple, out to its full extent, would have been useful information.

Still, if we haven't seen the last of him, if he decides that I was such a pushover the first time, that I'm worth another go in Glasgow, I'll know how to deal with him.

I do sympathise though. I would hate to lose Sharon.

★

We end up taking the chairs into the back garden –where I, for one, don't feel the cold, if there is any –so that Kirsty can smoke. Sharon accepts a cigarette when the packet is proffered.

'I'm just a casual smoker,' she explains to me, almost guiltily. 'I have one when I'm drinking, if someone's handing them out, that's all.'

'The worst and richest kind of casual smoker,' Kirsty accuses her mockingly. 'And she's drinking my wine. Angela and her mates were always into my stuff.'

'Is that why the dope always disappeared so fast when you were looking after it?' asks Jacqui.

'No, that's because I was a greedy girl; always rolling one up and sneaking down to an empty guest room in the dead of night.

'I'm alive, aren't I? Do you think I would've been if telltale Angela had known I had hash in the house?'

She means it as a throwaway comment, but for the rest of us, it darkens the conversation.

'Kirsten,' says Sharon awkwardly, 'Angie told us all about that. It must've been awful for you; I know it was for her. As far as someone like me can even understand what it must've been like, I mean.'

Kirsty gazes into her Benson and Hedges smoke for a few seconds.

'I can still get angry, even now I know she's dead.' She drains her glass and reaches for the bottle. 'I've hardly thought about anything but her and Grandad and the past today, and that's still how I feel sometimes: angry with her. When I drove past Callum Brae, on the way into town...

'But the thing is, Sharon, when something's in your past, you just about accept it in the end, no matter how bad it is. Well, some people don't, but then it controls their whole life. Well, only I control my life, which is a bloody good life now, even if I've been homeless, briefly, and threatened with really serious violence once, and locked in a cell half of every day for—Shit! You're Angela's friend. You better promise me right now you'll never tell her that.'

'Course I won't, if you don't want me to.'

I'm glad that this has come out in front of Sharon. I won't have to be constantly on my guard about mentioning it without thinking, now.

'Thanks,' says Kirsty. 'At least Grandad'll never know. Maybe I wouldn't really've cared if my mother had.'

'Is that where you've been most of the time?' Sharon asks cautiously.

'No, I didn't go in for murder. I might though, if you ever tell Angela.'

'Kirsty!' Jacqui and I protest simultaneously.

'It's all right, you two. Ask your sister whether I can keep a secret, Kirsten. It was always Jess who couldn't.

'And you're so right. If I promised not to tell, then I did, you'd have every right to kick my arse.'

Kirsty offers her another cigarette.

'Do you really work in the PF's Office in Glasgow?

'What a laugh; I'll be on file there somewhere. You can look up the details for yourself, I'm sick of talking about this shit. What's something interesting we can talk about?'

'Big dicks,' suggests Jacqui.

Kirsty shakes her head.

'Frightening to think she's the mother of girls. Really cool girls too, if I didn't say so earlier. Even if Donald is their father. You can't have developed this unhealthy interest of yours through being married to him, Mrs Shaw. Unless that's the point: dwelling on what you were missing.'

'His was fine,' says Jacqui defensively. 'You'll have forgotten. He's a lousy father and obviously not a great husband, or he'd be here, but I'll not have him criticised where it's not merited.'

'Not that size is important, of course,' quotes Kirsty, tongue in cheek, 'it's what they do with it.'

'Bullshit!' snorts Jacqui. 'Never mind what they do with it – it's size that matters, every time.'

'There have to be better subjects than this,' I comment.

'You would say that,' Jacqui grins. 'Name one.'

'Films?' I suggest at random. 'What's everybody's favourite? Mine's *Casablanca*, if I have to pick just one.'

'Really?' says Sharon. 'Despite everything there's been since?'

'No, but that was an amazing period in film making' Kirsty Supports me. '*Citizen Kane* may be overrated, but yeah, *Casablanca* is brilliant, and *Gone With the Wind*'s my all time favourite.'

'I never knew that,' Jacqui tells her.

'Nor did I when I was fifteen, it was probably *Flashdance* back then. But that incredible performance by Vivienne Leigh. Her and Garbo have to be the most talented, good-looking women who ever lived.'

'Aw, come on, let's not start raving about girls,' objects Jacqui. 'I wanted us to get drunk and say rude, disgusting things about men, like they're just sex objects, as if we were teenagers again.'

'We'll get to that, but let me finish. She drives me mad, Scarlett does – and Rhett, they're both as bad – but she's brilliantly portrayed, and a great character, if you suspend your disbelief. Hard to credit that she could go through everything she went through though, and still be using no stronger language by the end of the film than "fiddledeedee."'

'What else would a Southern belle have been likely to say, back then?' I ask.

'Well, be realistic. She was a grown woman, who'd been through loads of shit. You'd think she'd've said "fiddledeefuckingdee" now and again.'

★

Sharon is getting her mobile out to call us a taxi. We have all been drinking as though we're expecting the Scottish parliament to declare a state of prohibition at any moment.

Jacqui tears herself away from a walk down Memory Lane, where Kirsty is resurrecting her Italian at a party persona, and says;

'No way. There's loads of blankets upstairs. Just sleep on the floor. It'll be light in a few hours, anyway.'

So it is that I end up dossing down on the lounge carpet beside my girlfriend, with my ex snoring away on the couch.

Kirsty didn't used to snore. She must be over-tired from her long day and all that driving.

Coffee Morning

I wake up gradually the next morning. Ultimately, it's a pressing need to visit the toilet that propels me into action. I open my eyes and, hesitating only to admire Sharon in repose, crawl out from under the blankets, grab my top clothing and flee up to the bathroom.

Here I have to wait, as the door is locked. Who's in there? I've been listening to Jacqui and Carol's voices, floating through from the kitchen, so perhaps it's Natalie.

I've finished dressing by the time the cistern sounds. Following much running of taps, Kirsty emerges.

'Hello,' she smiles.

'Morning.'

'Who'd ever've thought it: us waking up under the same roof again?'

'But that time,' I remind her, 'I had new gear on hand to change into. Now it's welcome back to last night's clothing.'

'Not entirely, in my case. I've got clean knickers on.'

I shouldn't find the comment titillating; she did not intend me to.

'After driving here from Leicester in whatever you had on yesterday, I imagine that's a good thing, from where you're standing.'

'By now, it's probably even a good thing from where you're standing,' she says, starting down the staircase. 'I think they'll have to be ceremonially burnt later on, for everybody's sake.'

When I arrive back in the lounge, she's on the couch drinking coffee, Sharon is on top of our blankets, unselfconsciously doing the same thing in her underwear, and Jacqui is opening the curtains.

'On the table, Tim.'

I select one of the two steaming mugs which have been placed there. The bells of Saint Andrew's begin to ring as I pick it up, and for a moment, I suspect that I have triggered an extremely elaborate alarm system.

'Just off, Mum,' Carol announces, poking her head around the doorframe. She notices Sharon and wolf whistles.

'Stay right where you are, young lady,' glowers Jacqui menacingly, beginning to rise from the chair in which she has just deposited herself.

Carol disappears and we hear the back door slam.

'I am really going to have to take her in hand,' her mother tells us.

'She's fine,' says Kirsty. 'She's only reacting off us: the sort of things I say and those of us who enjoy flaunting our bodies.'

'She isn't showing proper respect for adults.'

This has been a fairly regular theme during my time in their house.

'It's good that she's a bit cheeky,' argues Kirsty. 'Shows character, proves she's got self-confidence. You could've done to be more like that at her age. She's a bit like I was.'

'That's really reassuring, Kirsty.'

'Hey, that's supposed to be my line. Know what you mean, though. I dread Melissa turning out like me. More like Mike so far, thank God.'

'I don't hit them, you know,' Jacqui informs her.

'I never thought you would. I've never touched Melissa or David.'

'Your son David,' says Jacqui. 'Is his middle name Sandy, by any chance?'

Kirsty smiles at her.

'Alexander, yeah. My tribute to Grandad, that and your tattoo.'

Why didn't I make that connection for myself? What greater significance does a poppy have than the killing fields of France and Flanders?

'Too bad I never got round to telling him about it. You can't exactly show your grandfather something in a place like that, but I should've told him. Didn't think he'd approve of a girl with a tattoo though, whatever it represented. He always thought of them as something mainly sailors had, and he couldn't stand sailors.'

'Where've the girls gone?' I ask, after we've all drunk our coffee in silence for half a minute.

'Carol just went to her friend Courtney's. Natalie's at Sunday school with her friend, also called Courtney.'

'Is that still going these days?' Sharon enquires in surprise, 'Sunday School?'

'Yeah, she loves it. She's the sort of girl who enjoys those structured sort of environments.'

'It's good to be back where people pronounce words like "girl" properly,' comments Kirsty.

'But she doesn't,' I say provocatively. 'She mangles it into two syllables and mispronounces it "gerrell" same as you two do.'

Somebody rings the doorbell, interrupting the flow of invective which is coming my way. Sharon slides back beneath the blankets and Jacqui answers the call, making a remark, as she does so, which is deeply disrespectful to all English-born people.

'Oh, hello,' she says warmly, to her English-born visitor. 'Come in.'

'Thanks.' Rex steps into the room. 'Bloody hell! It's like the morning after in a knocking shop.'

'Rex!' I bark at him.

'It's all right, we can take a joke,' simpers Jacqui. Well, not quite simpers, perhaps, but close. 'That would've been polite, coming from my ex-husband.'

Emphasis on the ex.

'Would've passed for the height of good manners in the squat and hostels I've lived in too,' says Kirsty, but more sarcastically.

'Yes, but this isn't a squat or a hostel,' I point out, 'so the height of good manners isn't quite so easy to reach.'

'I can see why you like it here,' Rex winks at me, 'brunette, blonde, redhead.'

'I remember now,' cries Kirsty. 'He's your brother. You had a brother living here called Rex, didn't you? Footballer.'

'You're Rex Wharton? Oh my God!'

Sharon has been staring at him in disbelief ever since he walked in. I was wondering why.

'Tim, you never said your brother was called Rex.'

'Is this a wind up?' he asks suspiciously.

'No,' she all but screams, 'I support Sheffield United – always have. Them and Aberdeen, same as my dad. My brother supported Rangers; he used to get *Shoot* and I used to nick all the Sheffield and Aberdeen pictures out of it. You were my second favourite player back then. I wanted to visit you when I first heard you'd moved up here, but I didn't dare.'

Rex is grinning from ear to ear. This can't have happened to him in sixteen years or longer.

'Don't tell me who your favourite was. There were some real prats in that squad.'

'You've hardly changed,' says Sharon breathlessly. 'I was thinking you had to be just someone who looked like you. I can't believe you're Tim's brother.'

'Wanner coffee, Rex?' Jacqui asks, in her sexy voice, which I have very recently identified as the one that she uses when he's around.

'Lovely, thanks. Tiny bit of milk, no sugar.'

He plops down on the couch beside Kirsty, with Sharon not far from his feet. She can't take her eyes off him. If this was a cartoon, her pupils would be heart shaped.

I'm making allowances for it being good, old-fashioned hero worship, which she will grow out of as she gets to know him as a person. Actually, I'm counting on it.

It doesn't help that Sharon's interest in him as a player was sure to have had adolescent sexual attraction as one of its motivations. She told me the other night that, in her early teens, she fancied just about anybody. Even Rex manages to meet that criterion.

'Do you still follow Sheffield United?' she asks him.

'Only in the sense that they're part of the game overall. Don't like the way they play.'

'Oh.'

An early hint of disillusionment? Hope so.

'I prefer rugby, myself,' says Kirsty.

Her attitude toward Rex differs greatly from that of the other two. He would have to actually do something worthwhile to impress her, not just sit around being Rex.

'Sorry,' I say, realising how remiss I've been, 'Rex, this is

Sharon and this is Kirsty.'

'Kirsty Crow?'

He is taken aback by this possibility.

'God, I'm world famous as well.'

'Yes, we managed to track her down.'

'Sorry to hear about what happened at the boarding house,' he says, shaking her hand. 'Must've been a terrible shock.'

'Yes.'

Kirsty leaves it at that.

He extends his hand to Sharon. If she pulls it under the blankets, she'll have to be spoken to later.

She shakes demurely, without even a: 'Wow! Rex Wharton's hand' to sully things. Then she stands up, taking the blankets with her, grabs her clothing and announces that she's going upstairs to change.

'Remember not to wash that hand,' Kirsty calls after her.

Rex looks at her with a definite something in his eye. Respect, I think. Maybe she's the one he fancies, because she isn't knocked out by his barely faded good looks or his very faded name.

'It's not easy being a has been, you know,' he tells her.

'I imagine not.'

'They're always pestering me to go on celebrity quiz shows.'

She smiles.

'When did you get back?' I ask.

'Last night. Thought I'd better come and track you down in your den of iniquity. Not that I knew it was one, 'til now.'

'Coffee,' announces Jacqui, sashaying into the room with her skirt hitched right up. Well, she's wearing three-quarter length trousers, but they've got a hitched up look, if anything has.

'Thanks,' Rex says. 'I bet that's another reason you like it here – great waitress service.'

'I don't get that all the time,' I assure him.

'Visitor service only,' Jacqui explains. 'My daughters and the regulars need to be able to look after themselves.'

'God, yeah, you don't wait on your kids,' Kirsty agrees.

'I did for a few years, but then I had to get tough about it.'

Jacqui begins to gather up empty mugs. She resists any temptation to wiggle as she passes close to Rex and disappears back into the kitchen.

Kirsty gets up and follows her, just as Sharon returns, with a neatly folded pile of blankets.

'How's your leg these days, Rex?'

'Completely better,' he replies. 'Now I'm thirty-nine and too old to make an earth shattering comeback.'

He's sending himself up. I'd never have expected to hear this. In 1986, it would've been impossible.

I drain my mug and take it straight to the kitchen where I find Kirsty and Jacqui holding a whispered consultation.

'Go on, just ask him. It's obvious you want to.'

'I don't want to. I'm fine.'

'You owe it to yourself. All those years with Don; you've got to move on.'

'I have moved on.'

'No, I mean—'

'I know what you mean, Kirsty, and I have, not long after he left me. I'm quite sure I will again sometime, when it just happens, or I meet someone I really want to be with.'

'Really? You mean you've technically committed adultery?'

'That's a bit of a pointless way of looking at it,' I interject.

Kirsty beams.

'Not to me, it isn't. This is maybe the first time she's done something I never have.'

'I hope you don't let it change your life, Jacqui,' I warn her.

'You should've seen us in our teens,' says Kirsty, no longer bothering to whisper, now that they have ceased discussing Rex. 'We were like a couple of Catholic girls. I was the one who tried everything and she was the type who didn't go too far on first dates and thought that when an act sounded disgusting, that was a reason to avoid it, instead of checking it out to make sure.'

'We're even now,' declares Jacqui, light-heartedly. 'You've given Tim the low-down on me, and that's exactly what I did on you about a week ago.'

'What? My colourful past?'

'Multicoloured, I've always thought. Is that what the dress symbolises?'

'Tell you what,' Kirsty suggests to me. 'If you want to know the bits I didn't even tell my best friend, you could try reading the walls of the men's toilets in town, if they haven't been repainted yet.'

'Right,' Rex calls from the lounge, 'now I remember where I've heard of you before.'

We all look at one another and laugh.

'He's starting to grow on me,' Kirsty's back to whispering, 'and that's another secret.'

'So when are you making for Auchtermuchty?' Jacqui asks her, as we wander into the lounge.

'I ought to go about now, really, if I'm going to have a decent bit of time with them before I need to be back on the road properly. At least they won't make me pay for the privilege of crossing that bridge, this way on.'

'Sorry, I forgot,' says Sharon, 'I do have some dim memory of promising to get Angie's address out of my diary for you, last night, don't I?'

'Thanks a lot.'

Even as Sharon picks up her handbag, it begins to bleep.

'Rafferty.'

I avoid catching Kirsty' s or Rex's eye.

'Oh, hi, this is amazing, I was just talking – thinking about you.

'What? Oh, there's no need to ring me on my mobile to thank me for that. This must be costing you the earth, ringing round instead of sending thank you cards. How's your dad now?

'Yeah? How about you?

'Look, Angie, I've lost your address. Thanks, I'll just get a pen.'

She puts her entire hand over the phone and says; 'Wanner talk to your sister?'

'No, I'd rather do this face to face,' Kirsty replies. 'Thanks for being so discreet.'

'Told you I was.'

'You've definitely got a good one there,' says Kirsty, as Sharon digs out a pen and note pad and moves further away. 'Give her a penis and she'd be perfect.'

'We often are, with those,' agrees Rex.

Kirsty sighs.

'Why do we risk releasing sportsmen back into the community?

'Nice day out there. I need a smoke.'

'Got a spare one?' requests Rex.

We end up drifting out towards the cars, Kirsty's small overnight bag in her hand. Linda used to take twice that amount on a day trip. Perhaps travelling light and cutting and running are skills which, if learnt at a formative age, remain with one.

'I'll get going too,' decides Sharon. 'Coming for some clean clothes, Tim? We can catch Jacqui and the girls again this afternoon.'

'No, hang on,' says Rex, removing the cadged Benson and Hedges from his mouth. 'I need you to come over to the cottage for a while. Won't take long.'

'All right,' I agree. 'You have the first shower, Sharon.'

'Okay. Give Angie my love, Kirsten.'

'Didn't you just give her it on the phone?'

'Probably. But I love Angie to bits.'

'This is getting a bit soppy for me,' Rex says. 'I'll wait in the car.

'You have a safe journey and I'll see you later.'

'Yeah, 'bye,' replies Kirsty distractedly. 'Sharon, can I be personal?'

'Yes.'

'How does my sister handle being loved to bits by a friend who kicks with both feet?'

Sharon's beautiful slow smile creeps up her cheekbones.

'You must've wondered. I didn't tell her for ages, then when I did, she was pretty shocked, but still a decent enough person to know that friendship's friendship, even when one of you's straight and one's bisexual.'

She kisses Kirsty on the cheek, me on the mouth and gets into her car.

'Now let's cut out the middle woman.' Kirsty puckers her lips at me. 'I'm saving Jacqui for last.'

This could sound highly suggestive to the neighbours.

We kiss briefly on the mouth. Mike, I decide, is almost as lucky as I am.

This may be as final as our last parting was supposed to be. It's anybody's guess whether we will coincide on weekend visits to Jacqui in the months and years ahead. One of us ought to organise a reunion of last night's gathering sometime.

'What was Tim short for again?' Kirsty asks, as I make for the four-wheel drive.

'Timothea.'

'That's right. Unusual…'

'Horrible,' I say. 'My mum read it somewhere and liked it. I wasn't putting up with that.'

'Cool,' approves Kirsty. 'Deciding that if women could run round calling themselves Sam and Charley and all the rest, you could do the same.'

'Suits you somehow,' says Jacqui.

'I'll be bringing the family up here soon,' Kirsty informs me, 'so we may meet again another day.'

'Tomorrow's another day,' I remind her.

'Fiddledeefuckingdee,' she says.

Tim

She was a blast from my past, but now I'm going to have a new life. With Sharon. Living together openly. A first for me.

Before Linda, there was the Old Man. I wouldn't have dared come out with him alive, not before the age of nineteen, when he died, anyway. Then the reputation of the shop had to be considered, although I told my mum and Rex during that time. She was very supportive, as my stepfather Joe has been, despite her disappointment. Rex wasn't crazy about having a gay sister, but perhaps he expected little better from me by then. My ruining the business was what truly bothered him.

There were friends who already knew, and others whom I met and took into my confidence as time went by. People I could trust, such as Mandy and Bob. Still I did not completely go public.

Linda came along and then I was ready to. I wanted us to be together and didn't care who knew. She did. Now there was her business to worry about. She argued that women would not want to buy underwear from somebody whom they might suspect of trying to imagine them in it, hence the fact that men were never employed to sell it. She might have been right, we didn't put it to the test. There again, Linda hasn't even told her family.

So she eventually broke up with me, not for the first time, but it has turned out to be the last. She wants to be straight, if only for commercial reasons. She isn't even bisexual, she's just in a closet, one in which I was keeping her company, and she thinks that she can make it work with a man, because sex isn't everything and she doesn't hate the penetrative act.

She wants to get married. She has been terrified, for a long time, that the lingerie buying public will simply presume lesbianism if she remains single indefinitely. I would imagine that many people have suspected for ages that she and I were an item. It would have been contrary to my own interests to share that theory with her though.

I wouldn't count on it, but she may even have a successful marriage, perhaps with children, perhaps without. So long as her husband understood. Not about her sexuality, she wouldn't complicate things by bringing that up. So long as he understood that the most important aspect of her life, which will always take up most of her energy and passion, is Knickerlodeon.

By chasing Kirsty, as a reaction to being dumped, I have found Sharon, and the exciting, scary challenge that is offered by Glasgow. Then there's Jacqui – a new, totally accepting friend, for this part of the world – and Carol and Natalie. And I'm getting it back together with Rex. I hope that Kirsty is able to work something like that out with what remains of her family. That will make this trip of mine even more worthwhile.

Echoing In The Shadows

As we drive along the coast road, Rex asks; 'You and that redhead involved then?'

'Sharon, yeah. I'm going back to Glasgow with her tonight and we're gonner see how it works out.'

'Hope it does then,' says Rex. 'You know, I never thought I'd walk into a roomful of women and you'd've had more of them than me. Two-nil, that's impressive. You'd never know it to look at those two.'

'Jacqui's straight.'

'Yeah, right – as you no doubt found out the hard way.'

We'll leave it at that then. I don't want to try more blatantly matchmaking them; I've always thought that intrusive, and I do have reservations about Rex being what Jacqui truly needs.

'So you and Sharon are giving it a go, are you?'

'Despite legal intervention to stop it, yes.'

I tell him the story of Greg.

'Find out where he lives. I'll soon convince him he should leave my sister alone.'

'It's all right, Sharon's done that, and more effectively than anyone else could.'

Fraternal over-protectiveness is not something that I suddenly have a need for.

'Oh, I can be effective,' promises Rex.

'No, thanks.'

The sun's out again today, sparkling on the sea. I wonder if it ever gets so hot here that swimming in it is an irresistible temptation?

'Any developments while I was away, with Kirsty's grandfather and mother?' Rex enquires.

'Nothing they're telling us about yet. The investigation is proceeding; I suppose they'd say.

'I'm pretty sure I was wrong now. It must've been a burglar.

Or some enemy of Isla's I know nothing about. Kirsty didn't kill her and she certainly didn't kill Kirsty. I'm sure Jess at Seaview didn't do it, even if she did hate her. Or Angela, or her husband, or Kirsty's husband, or anyone else who might've borne Isla a grudge for beating up her daughters.'

'Pretty unlikely, I suppose.'

'No, when they do make an arrest, it'll be someone none of us have heard of. Maybe Isla did cross somebody.'

This idea is growing on me.

'The real pity is that old Sandy had to get in the way. Typical Isla: harming a member of her family even when she got herself killed.'

'Still, it brought the prodigal daughter back,' Rex reminds me. 'Took me by surprise when I realised who she was. Didn't know what to say to her.'

We arrive at his pink stone cottage and swing into the drive, temporarily turning our backs on the seascape.

'Beer?' Rex offers, as I seat myself on his couch, enjoying the view once more.

'God, no.' Last night's excesses have left me with a lingering aftertaste. I've known worse, but I also know better; better, at least, than to drink again at eleven-fifteen the next morning.

'You're probably right,' he agrees, taking an armchair. 'And we've both had enough coffee for now.'

'So what was it you wanted exactly?' I ask. 'And what've you been doing in Edinburgh? Getting laid?'

'Well, yeah, but that was just coincidental. Unlike you, it's not the reason I'm moving on. Tomorrow, actually.'

'What?'

'I've been organising a flight back to Sydney. Fly out of Manchester on Wednesday.'

'Oh.' This is a bolt from the blue, but there's a pleasing side to it. 'That's good, you'll be able to spend time with your kids again.'

'Yeah, I've missed them the whole time I've been here. They're not the only reason, but—'

'What about Mum though?' If he's going to slope off without seeing her... 'I need to speak to her by tomorrow.'

'Leave it 'til the evening then and you can speak to me too. I'll be spending a day or so there on my way.'

'Oh that's great, Rex. She'll be over the moon. And hey, you'll like Joe.'

'I'll try my best to,' he tells me. 'How'd you like the use of this place?'

'What do you mean?'

'Well, you and that sexy little thing can come here for weekends, save you having to stay with her parents, if they'd even let you. Or if you two don't work out, you could move over here, if you didn't want to go back home.'

'Thanks for being so confident about us but, yeah, it'd be great as a weekend retreat.'

'A but and ben,' Rex grins. 'Done then. I'll be in touch about which account you can pay the rates out of.'

'Be happy to.'

'Then there's the car. I'll leave that at Mum's. You'll be going down to tie up your loose ends soon, I suppose, so you can take it back to Glasgow then.'

I can't believe that he's being so generous, but this is overdoing it. Besides, I can't be seen dead in a four-wheel drive.

'Rex, you can't give me your car.'

'Call it an indefinite loan. Or if you really can't do it and want to put it up for sale for me, fine, but use it while you're advertising it. Even in Glasgow there's got to be someone who wants a decent vehicle.'

'This is all very sudden,' I say.

'Same as the idea of you staying in Scotland is. Strange how it works out, isn't it? I came to live here because it's where Grandma's from, but I've never quite managed to stay. You come up because of me and meet Kirsty. Then you come back looking for her and find me. And Sharon. There's a lot of cause and effect going on here. More than you'd realise.'

'Do you know about cause and effect?' I ask in surprise.

Rex grimaces and gazes out across the turquoise sea.

'You don't have to be thick as two short planks to kick a ball decently, you know. You were never too bad a player, for a... you weren't too bad, and you're not stupid. Sure, intelligent players aren't necessarily intelligent guys, but we weren't all interested in nothing outside the game apart from nightclubs, shagging and golf. Look at Eric Cantona: poetry, philosophy, painting, acting. To be honest, I actually prefer golf and shagging to most of those things, except philosophy, maybe, but you get my point. Those aren't my main interests in life and I respect other players who go for something other than the most obvious pastimes.'

'Sorry.' I would never seriously question his intelligence, but he seems to have become a deeper thinker than of yore, since mellowing and mediocrity began their work. 'Not that I know what your main interests in life actually are.'

'Yes, you do. The game still, to an extent. This place. Family. You know, Dad's side. Researching the history of it, especially the Scots.'

How ironic. That limited concept of family is so important to him, that he has been prepared to leave his own children on the other side of the world so that he can breathe daily the air of our grandmother's birthplace and have immediate access to local parish records.

At least he has realised his mistake and is doing what it takes to put it right.

'I'll miss it here,' he says quietly. 'But it's for the best.'

'Absolutely.'

'I need you to do me another favour though.'

'Just name it.'

Look at everything he's doing for me.

'I want you to let me know any developments in this Crow case. Keep your eye on it through Jacqui or someone. Maybe that boarding house keeper who knows a cop.'

'Yeah, if you like. Why?'

Rex looks straight at me.

'I killed them.'

This is tasteless. I need to know that it's tasteless.

There is something about the way he said it that I don't like.

'That's not funny, Rex.'

'I know. I'm not joking.'

Reality has ceased to exist. I had finally found myself a highly acceptable reality and now I've lost it. Perhaps for good.

'You didn't know them,' I shout. 'How can you expect me to

believe that you killed someone you hadn't met?'

'There is a reason.'

'Like what?'

He has to be insane. He either thinks that he did it, or he actually did, and either way, that makes him a raving nutter.

'That old bastard,' says Rex, 'killed our great grandfather.'

'What the bloody hell are you talking about?'

'Crow. Her grandfather. He killed Sergeant James Hay on July the first, 1916, in the middle of No Man's Land. Just after they went over the top on the Somme. Grandma Wharton's maiden name was Hay—'

'I know what her bloody maiden name was. I don't need a family history lesson from you, however much you think you know. I know where he died. Her mother married a veteran and moved down to Yorkshire so he—'

'And I don't need a family history lesson from you,' he snaps. 'Did she tell you he was murdered by a soldier on his own fucking side?'

'Course she didn't. I don't know where you've got hold of such a ridiculous story.'

'Ridiculous story? You're the one who put the pieces together for me, telling me Crow had murdered his sergeant on the first day of the Somme. Local pals' battalion. What were the odds?'

It was me? I was the catalyst that set this horror story in motion?

'I used to ring Grandma from Oz quite a lot,' explains Rex. 'I was often homesick in the early days and I was always pumping her for family history. She told me a few juicy things. She was a bit reluctant with that story and said she didn't want it spreading round the family if I ever got back in touch; said there'd never been any proof and it wasn't something she'd even told Dad about.

'Apparently, a soldier dying gradually of his wounds had a letter he'd dictated smuggled out of France by an orderly going home on compassionate leave. It'd never have got past the censor any other way. He knew Great-Grandma Hay, that soldier; he used to work with Great-Grandad in a local distillery, closed down now. Said he wanted her to know the truth about her husband, the truth about the war. He wasn't prepared to name names, but James Hay had been shot by one of his own men, for personal reasons. Personal reasons…' Rex curls his upper lip derisively. 'So when you told me about that old man perched up there, bragging to his granddaughter about it…'

'It wasn't like that.'

'Oh no? So what was it fucking like then?'

'If anything,' I tell him, 'it sounds exactly the same as Grandma telling you. Something told in confidence, this seventy-year-old secret.'

And never should the twain have met. If not for me connecting them.

'I just wanted to hear him admit to it really,' Rex continues, 'I went to Callum Brae, explained I was your brother and would really like to meet a World War One vet. She let me in, took me up, told me to speak loudly and left us to it.

'I told him who I was, then just asked him if the man he shot on July the first, 1916, was called Sergeant Hay. You can imagine the look on his disgusting old face. "Your sister can't have told you that," he said, "I didn't tell Kirsty his name." What more did I need to hear?

'I asked him why. He said; "he made my life hell. I don't know who he was to you, but I maybe did him a favour; he might've died of his injuries bit by bit, the next couple of days – that's how long it often took the stretcher bearers to get out to the wounded at the beginning of the Somme." "That's not why you did it though, was it?" I said. "It wasn't a mercy killing." He said; "no, I'd never've shown that bastard mercy."

'That did it. He was so fucking cocky; like, for all he knew, I could've been secretly taping him, but it didn't matter, because he'd probably be dead by the time it got to court. Just another old murderer, like Pinochet and those bastards from the concentration camps, who think their age gives them power, and really they're not powerful at all, and just need one person who's prepared to come along and show them that.

'I pushed him against the wall, that was all. Hard. He died straightaway. Barely made a sound. I knew there was no point checking his pulse.'

'He was a hundred and fucking six!'

'He killed our great grandfather,' Rex cries.

'And did you ever think,' I demand, 'what a bastard this ancestor of ours must've been, to inspire so much hatred in somebody whose side he was supposed to be on?'

'Not ancestor, you silly cow; we were all alive in the same century, only a few decades apart.'

'Fifty years.'

'He was a member of our family, fighting for king and country. Look at the long life his killer's had. Where's the natural justice?

'Look at all the decent people who must've died of cancer and heart attacks since that arsehole lived past his sell by date and just kept on living. Look at Dad, dead at forty-eight.

'I tell you, I'm never letting my life drag out like that. It's bad enough getting to this age and not being able to get from one end of a pitch to the other the way I could a few years back.'

A realisation hits me almost as hard as anything else that he's said so far.

'You killed Isla too?'

Rex smiles.

'You and the police got it arse about face. She was the one who just got in the way. I was standing looking down at him and she suddenly just came into the room. I could see in her face that she knew he hadn't just died and fallen out of his seat. She stood there looking at me; she'd hardly started to run when I grabbed her. I threw her down the stairs. I wanted to make sure of her, not have to end up strangling her, or finishing her off with some blunt instrument I'd have to dispose of afterwards.

'From what you've told me, she deserved it.'

'You didn't know that at the time.'

'No,' he admits. 'Shit, the noise she made going down! I hadn't been thinking straight; I realised I didn't know for sure that her husband wasn't around, or the odd guest. If anyone else appeared, I knew I was fucked. You can't just keep knocking them off one after the other.

'But there wasn't anybody else. It soon became obvious I was alone in the house with two dead people.

'I got my hanky out, wiped everything I could remember touching. Opened the back door with it over my hand. That was okay, it was private round the back there, but getting out the yard gate into the snicket, shit, that took some doing. Stood listening for ages, then I opened it, with my hanky, peered round it. Nobody there, so I was off. Forced myself not to run. I only remembered to take my hanky off my hand and put it away before I was about to step into the street. But it seems like nobody noticed me at all'.'

So there it is. A first-hand account of double homicide.

'Are you round the bend, telling me this?'

'No,' he replies mildly. 'I know I can trust you. And I need someone back here to keep an ear to the ground. I can't swear I got every single fingerprint in there. Mine aren't on file, and I'll be going over every millimetre of this place tomorrow, as well as the car, before I leave it. But you can't be too careful. At least if I'm in Oz, they won't be able to just come and grab me.'

The real reason he's going back.

'They can extradite you from there, in case you didn't know.'

'That's why I need you here,' he says. 'One word from you and I can be on a plane to South America. I just need to get money ready in offshore accounts. I know how corny it must sound; I wouldn't want to end up like Ronald Biggs, having to marry a Brazilian woman or get one pregnant, just so you can stay there. Still, it's one continent where I'd surely be able to get a football-coaching job, and if the worst came to the worst, it'd be a lot better than the alternative. I'm not going down for lowlifes like those fucking Crows.'

'Where do you get the nerve to just presume I'll help you?' I ask him in amazement. 'You hadn't seen me in years until ten odd days ago, don't kid yourself you bloody know me. Why should I even keep your crime a secret? I'm in a relationship with somebody whose friend's mother and grandfather were murdered by you. And Kirsty was very fond of Sandy. Why do you think I'd put you first?'

'Do you want to upset Kirsty?' demands Rex.

'No. Why would I? She's been through enough.'

'Then don't let her realise that she caused his death, by telling you that he killed our great grandfather. Cause and effect, see?

'Stupid old sod. I wouldn't trust a mouthy blonde like that with anything I wanted kept quiet. Actually, I could think of lots of better things to do with her than talk.'

'She's not—' I say, then stop. Let her be a blonde, in his fantasy. Between the geographical separation and her morality, he's never going to get up close and personal enough to realise the truth.

Kirsty spent a year in prison for next to nothing. This arsehole expects to get away with two murders, and has the wealth to make it a possibility, if the finger of suspicion is ever pointed in his direction.

'Unfortunately for you,' I say, 'I've got my own ideas about natural justice too. I can't see why you should get off.'

Rex snorts.

'They'd never believe you. I'm a fairly respectable ex-footballer, who lives on my own means. You're a lesbian social security scrounger, who might just be a man hater who can't stand her own brother.'

'I wouldn't bank on the police thinking that way in this century. Not all of them.'

'I'm not. I'm banking on you not turning me in for Mum's sake. She'll've only just got to know me again. Think what me being put away would do to her.'

The bastard. I know he's right. I can't imagine convincing myself that he isn't, that it doesn't matter.

'And that's why you're going to see her tomorrow,' I accuse him, 'ingratiating yourself.'

He shrugs.

'We do what we have to, don't we?'

'What we have to?'

I think about a woman flying down a staircase, about a frail old man being effortlessly executed for something that he did eighty-seven years ago.

'To look after ourselves,' clarifies Rex. 'I've had to do that for myself for a long time now. Dad was the only one who ever did it for me. Nobody else. You know why the FA's called the FA? 'Cause that's all they do for young players who are just unlucky.

The fans soon forget you after it's over, unless you're Stanley Matthews. And if he'd been out of the game at twenty-two, instead of fifty, there'd've been no minute's silence for him, no mention on the news.'

'You wanner be on the news, just step down to the police station in town,' I suggest.

'You'd like to see that happen to your wonderful mother and ex-girlfriend, would you?'

'No,' I stand up. 'So now you know. But I won't be using this cottage and I'm not helping you in any way.'

'Your choice,' he says casually. 'That's just the car you're taking then, is it?'

'You can drive your wanky fucking four-wheel drive over that cliff out there if you don't want it.'

He laughs as I turn away from him.

'See yourself out, if you could, please.'

I don't reply. I leave his house. I don't even slam the front door. But as soon as it's shut, I kick it so hard that I put a small dent in the wood.

He doesn't come out to investigate and my toe doesn't quite feel broken.

I limp away, my mind travelling at a much faster pace.

I think about 1916 and the first disastrous contact between two families, which has led to this. I think about Kirsty, Kirsty and me; the only significant meeting between a Crow and one of us which didn't culminate in murder.

I hope she's wrong. I hope I don't see her again, her or Auchtermuchty Angela, now that I know about this. I hope I can push it to the back of my mind as quickly as possible. But then, I've always hoped for a lot of things.

Still hobbling, I walk back along the cliff top towards the town.

Made in the USA
Lexington, KY
05 May 2011